Kelly couldn't
Trent...

The way he'd held on to her hand as they scaled the roof. Or the feel of his hands moving over her body as he gently checked her for injuries. She couldn't let her mind dwell on how he held her.

"I need to go out for a while before I do something we'll both regret," Trent said, looking so deep in her eyes that Kelly couldn't breath, couldn't move, couldn't do anything but stare back at him, knowing full well that the longing inside her was reflected in her eyes for him to see.

"You have to stop looking at me that way," he murmured, his face closer somehow or maybe it was her imagination. "I can't...not react."

Before she could stop herself, she touched him. She couldn't stop staring at his mouth. He took her chin between his thumb and forefinger, lifting her face up to his. That mesmerizing mouth swooped down on hers, kissing her like she'd never been kissed before.

There was no gentleness this time, no tender brushing of lips, this was passion personified....

Dear Harlequin Intrigue Reader,

Those April showers go hand in hand with a welcome downpour of gripping romantic suspense in the Harlequin Intrigue line this month!

Reader-favorite Rebecca York returns to the legendary 43 LIGHT STREET with *Out of Nowhere*—an entrancing tale about a beautiful blond amnesiac who proves downright lethal to a hard-edged detective's heart. Then take a detour to New Mexico for *Shotgun Daddy* by Harper Allen—the conclusion in the MEN OF THE DOUBLE B RANCH trilogy. In this story a Navajo protector must safeguard the woman from his past who is nurturing a ticking time bomb of a secret.

The momentum keeps building as Sylvie Kurtz launches her brand-new miniseries—THE SEEKERS—about men dedicated to truth, justice…and protecting the women they love. But at what cost? Don't miss the debut book, *Heart of a Hunter,* where the search for a killer just might culminate in rekindled love. Passion and peril go hand in hand in *Agent Cowboy* by Debra Webb, when COLBY AGENCY investigator Trent Tucker races against time to crack a case of triple murder!

Rounding off a month of addictive romantic thrillers, watch for the continuation of two new thematic promotions. A handsome sheriff saves the day in *Restless Spirit* by Cassie Miles, which is part of COWBOY COPS. *Sudden Recall* by Jean Barrett is the latest in our DEAD BOLT series about silent memories that unlock simmering passions.

Enjoy all of our great offerings.

Sincerely,

Denise O'Sullivan
Senior Editor
Harlequin Intrigue

AGENT COWBOY
DEBRA WEBB

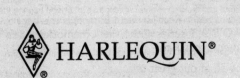

HARLEQUIN®

TORONTO • NEW YORK • LONDON
AMSTERDAM • PARIS • SYDNEY • HAMBURG
STOCKHOLM • ATHENS • TOKYO • MILAN • MADRID
PRAGUE • WARSAW • BUDAPEST • AUCKLAND

ISBN 0-373-22768-X

AGENT COWBOY

ABOUT THE AUTHOR

Debra Webb was born in Scottsboro, Alabama, to parents who taught her that anything is possible if you want it badly enough. When her husband joined the military, they moved to Berlin, Germany, and Debra became a secretary in the commanding general's office. By 1985 they were back in the States, and with the support of her husband and two beautiful daughters, Debra took up writing full-time and in 1998 her dream of writing for Harlequin came true. You can write to Debra with your comments at P.O. Box 64, Huntland, Tennessee 37345 or visit her Web site at www.debrawebb.com to find out exciting news about her next book.

Books by Debra Webb

*Colby Agency
**The Specialists

CAST OF CHARACTERS

Kelly Pruitt —She's on the run from the people who killed her boss. She can't trust the police or the FBI...can she trust the cowboy who shows up at her door?

Trent Tucker—As a Colby Agency investigator, it's Trent's job to find Kelly and to solve the mystery surrounding a multiple homicide and her disappearance. But can he keep her alive long enough to sort through the pieces of the puzzle?

Ray Jarvis—Kelly's boss. Is he laundering money for the cartel?

Ann Jones—Is she friend or foe? She took the bullet intended for Kelly. Did she invite murder into Kelly's life?

Cyrus McCade—The FBI special agent is running interference for the cartel. He wants Kelly Parker dead.

Norton Davis—Is the FBI special agent set up to take McCade's fall? Or is the twenty-five thousand dollars in his pocket an investment for his future?

William Lester—Is the senator trying to help a friend or bring down an old foe?

Detective Hargrove—Is he working for the investigation or against it?

Detective Kennamer—He's in it for the money.

Heath Murphy—Trent's backup from the Colby Agency.

Darlene Whitehead—Is she in love with Ray Jarvis or his money?

This book is dedicated to a lady who listens to me
whine when I'm worried; who says all the right things
when I think everything is going wrong; and who is
simply a good friend. To my agent, Pattie Steele-Perkins.
Thanks for being my sounding board.

Chapter One

Houston, Texas
Friday, 4:45 p.m.

Kelly Pruitt watched as her boss greeted his final appointment for the day at the front entrance of his small Houston office. A frown wriggled its way across her forehead. Something wasn't quite right about the scene playing out before her but she couldn't put her finger on the problem.

"Hold my calls," Ray Jarvis said to her as he ushered the client into his private office.

"Yes, sir."

Once the door was closed Kelly shrugged. She hadn't made the appointment. She hadn't even known her boss expected anyone else this close to five o'clock on Friday evening. He usually liked to get away a little early on Fridays. Especially since this one kicked off a long holiday weekend.

Happy New Year.

She certainly hoped the new year would see to fruition the fulfillment of all her boss had promised her. Kelly shuffled together a pile of "to be filed" records on her desk and decided that filing would be her final task for the day. She preferred leaving her desk uncluttered. Mondays seemed a little less daunting when she came in to a clean desk to start off the workweek.

As she moved from drawer to drawer, file folder to file folder, slipping in the relevant documents, she considered that she hadn't completed five years of college, including obtaining her MBA, to perform clerical duties in a small Houston investment firm. But, during her extensive job search, she had been forced to see the one major strike against her—youth. It seemed, she'd found out the hard way, that no one wanted to hire her in the position she was qualified for because she was only twenty-two. Graduating high school a year early and maintaining a perfect four-point-oh grade point average in college didn't matter in light of her lack of experience.

After searching for three solid months without the first bite, Raymond Jarvis finally offered her a job as his "administrative assistant." He promised her a junior partnership after one year of dedicated service, assuming she lived up to his expectations.

She, apparently, had done so. Ray had told her at Christmas that the upcoming year would be hers. In a show of good faith, he'd already started interviewing actual secretaries to take over the clerical duties.

A smile stretched across Kelly's face, erasing the frown that had nagged at her earlier. Very soon she would take her rightful place in the ever-changing

world of high finance. She couldn't wait. No more
monotonous filing, no more tedious reports, no—

"Kelly."

As she dropped the last record into the appropriate
folder, she looked up to find Ray emerging from his
office, then carefully closing the door behind him.

Before she could ask what he needed, he hurried
to where she stood by the long row of five-drawer
high file cabinets. "I need you to put this away some
place safe."

She accepted the small computer disk he offered.
"Does it pertain to a particular client's file?" She had
organized the computer disks the same as she had the
hard copies of files. Whoever took over would have
no problem following her system.

"Ah…" He gave the question entirely too much
consideration before answering. "No…just…ah…"

Was it her imagination or was he sweating? A new
line of concern formed along her brow. What in the
world had made her boss so antsy?

"Just take it home with you and lock it up with
your personal files."

"My personal files?" she echoed, surprised by the
suggestion. His gaze collided with hers and for just
one instant she recognized fear in his. "Ray, is—"

"If," he cut her off, the fear she'd seen in his eyes
vanishing in the same instant, "you don't mind. It's
just that if something happened here then those files
would be safe." He pressed her with his gaze, some
unreadable emotion making her suddenly uneasy.
"I'd really feel better about it if I knew you had a

copy safely tucked away. You might need it...some-time."

She nodded uncertainly. "All right. I'll take care of it."

He smiled to put her at ease, the expression clearly strained. "Don't bother waiting for me. The other offices in the complex have already closed. Lock up and go on home." He started to turn away but hesitated and glanced back at her. "Happy New Year."

She managed a dim smile. "Same to you."

When he'd gone back into his office and closed the door firmly behind him, she stared down at the disk. What on earth was this about? She'd worked for Ray for just over six months and she'd never seen him behave this way. Strange. Spooked, almost. He was always the epitome of cool and calm. His ability to make snap decisions under intense pressure never ceased to amaze her. What was it about this disk— her gaze shifted to his closed office door once more— and this client that made him so uncharacteristically agitated?

Kelly considered all that she'd noted about the client. Mid-thirties, she guessed. Well dressed in a charcoal suit. Dark hair. Not particularly handsome, but attractive in a generic, polished businessman sort of way. Nothing about him gave her pause—it was her boss's reaction to him that didn't fit. He hadn't even introduced her to the client and he never failed to do that.

Ray Jarvis prided himself on a family-like atmosphere at his place of business. He'd told her over and over again that he hadn't chosen an upscale office building downtown for that very reason. He preferred the smaller, more personal atmosphere of this quiet, off the beaten path, office complex. As he'd pointed out, his immediate neighbors, a mortgage company and an orthodontics office, had already closed for the weekend.

For the first time since she'd started working here, Kelly felt uneasy...alone. Somehow set apart from the rest of the world. It was completely ridiculous. Whatever was bugging Ray appeared to be contagious.

The bell over the front door jingled, drawing her from the troubling thoughts.

"Am I early?"

A genuine smile curled Kelly's lips as she greeted her friend, Ann Jones. "Definitely not." She felt better already just having another warm body in the room.

Ann, looking regal as always, came over and gave Kelly a hug. "That tyrant isn't planning to keep you late today, is he?" She glanced at Ray's closed door.

Kelly shook her head. Ann knew Ray was a pushover. "No. He's with a client. Just give me a couple minutes to finish clearing my desk and I'll be ready."

"Make it fast. I'm in a hurry to get started on this weekend."

Kelly laid the disk on her desk next to her purse and quickly sorted the messages Ray had yet to return. That annoying frown bored another line across her forehead. Why hadn't he taken care of his messages? He hadn't returned a single call all afternoon. There had to be something going on that she didn't know about. Maybe something had gone wrong in his personal life. But then she remembered distinctly that he'd told her earlier in the week that he and his girl-friend had big plans for the weekend. They were go-ing to New Orleans for the festivities. Maybe they'd broken up last night and he hadn't wanted to talk about it.

Kelly almost hated to leave under the circum-stances. She liked her boss, considered him a friend, as well. Maybe she should hang around and simply ask him if everything was okay.

"Can I use your phone?" Ann asked abruptly.

Kelly stepped aside and gestured to her desk. "Sure. I'll get my coat."

Ann reached across her desk and snatched up the receiver then swore. "Sorry," she muttered. "I think I knocked something off your desk."

The disk lay on the tile at Ann's feet. "I'll get it," Kelly said quickly. She should have put it in her purse already. Ray obviously considered it important.

Just as she crouched down to grab the disk, Ann shifted her stance and inadvertently knocked it be-neath the desk with the toe of her high-heeled shoe.

"Well, damn, Kelly, I'm sorry," she muttered as her fingers paused in their work of entering the tele-phone number she wished to call. She moved slightly aside, as far as the phone cord would allow. "I'm a real klutz today."

"No problem." Kelly eased onto all fours and crawled under her desk to retrieve the disk, all the while mentally kicking herself for not having put it away as soon as Ray gave it to her. Her fingers curled around the disk at the same moment that the bell over the front entrance jingled. She turned too quickly, banging her head against the desk's middle drawer. Cursing herself silently, she clenched her teeth a moment to allow the ache to pass. The modesty panel prevented her from seeing who'd entered the office so late on Friday. Surely there wasn't another appointment she didn't know about. Whoever it was she had every intention of letting him or her know that the office was now closed.

When she would have backed from under the desk an odd sort of pop hissed through the air. Rubbing her throbbing skull, Kelly stilled. What the hell?

Something plunked against the top of her desk and then struck her in the small of the back, sending her scooting fully under the desk to escape whatever had fallen. Irritation and impatience vying for equal footing she turned so she could see what had hit her. Before she could demand an explanation from Ann the sight of the phone receiver dangling over the edge of her desk silenced her.

Why was...

A blur of movement captured her attention, derailing her thoughts, as something else hit the floor.

It took three full seconds for Kelly to realize it was Ann. An ever-expanding circle of crimson engulfed her white blouse starting in the center of her chest.

Confusion obliterating all else, Kelly leaned forward for a closer look and her heart stalled in her chest.

Blood.

Her gaze jerked upward, to her friend's face. Her

brown eyes were open, unblinking, staring at the ceiling.

When Kelly would have scrambled from under the desk to help her friend, the sound of purposeful footsteps stopped her.

The thud of those heavy steps moved closer and closer to her desk. Kelly held her breath as booted feet and dark clad legs came into view. Big. Male. One black boot nudged Ann's motionless body but she didn't move, didn't react…those unblinking eyes glued to the ceiling.

Ann was dead.

The realization hit Kelly like a bullet between her eyes, straight into the brain. Dead. Ann was dead.

If you'd like to make a call, please hang up and try your call again.

The automated voice seemed to scream from the dangling telephone receiver. Kelly's eyes widened as fear mushroomed inside her. If he reached for the phone…would he see her? Every instinct urged her to draw more fully into herself, to press against the modesty panel in an attempt to get farther away from the threat.

But she didn't dare move.

A gloved hand reached for the receiver. The audible click told her he'd placed it in its cradle.

For two endless beats she waited for him to bend down and see her…to drag her from her hiding place. She didn't move, didn't even breathe.

And then he moved away. By the sound of his steps she knew he was moving toward Ray's office. A scream welled in her throat. She had to warn him! But if she moved…if she uttered a single word.

The door opened…banged against the wall.

More of those hissing pops.

Not a single protest was uttered.

Only the muffled sound of something falling to the carpeted floor of her boss's office. Ray…his client.

Then the stranger was moving about again.

Still in Ray's office.

She should run.

If she made it out onto the street she could scream for help.

But everyone else in the complex was already gone.

No one would hear her.

He—the man wearing the boots—would kill her, too.

As if he'd heard her thoughts he moved back into the corridor outside Ray's office…came closer to her desk.

She could feel her heart pounding against her sternum. *Please God,* she prayed, *don't let him know I'm here.* The blood roared so loudly in her ears she felt certain he could hear it…could feel the fear swelling inside her.

''It's done.''

She cocked her head and listened. Who was he talking to? He hadn't picked up the phone on her desk. No one else had come in. A cell phone…*maybe*.

''Jarvis and the assistant.'' Pause. ''Him, too. No survivors.''

Oh God. He had killed Ray and the client in his

office. Her eyes glazed with tears as her gaze settled on her friend. Ann. He thought Ann was...her. *The assistant.*

"I have the disk." Pause. "No. There are too many possibilities to assume this would be his only copy. I suggest you send in a team to tear this place apart."

Her fingers tightened around the disk in her hand.

"I'm doing that now." The whir of the blinds being lowered punctuated his statement. The lights went out next. "I'll be waiting out front."

In the eternity that followed, he moved through the entire suite, Ray's office, the lounge and rest room, the conference room, and then back into the lobby. The bob of a flashlight's beam accompanied his movements. He'd turned off all the lights and lowered all blinds. Her heart thundered so hard she wondered if a heart attack was imminent. Then she heard the whoosh of the front door as he exited the lobby.

That's when she started to shake.

He was gone. Outside. He'd told the man on the phone that he'd wait out front. A team was coming to tear the place apart.

She had to get out of here.

But how?

He was watching.

She licked her lips and gave her body the order to move. Yet it took several seconds before her muscles reacted.

Slowly, one inch at a time, she eased out from under the desk. She bumped into Ann's body and a moan tore from her lips. Kelly clamped a hand over her mouth and resisted the urge to heave. Hot tears streamed down her cheeks and over her hand.

Ann was dead.

Ray was dead.

So was the unidentified client.

She had to get out…to run!

Slowly, careful not to make a sound, Kelly crawled away from the desk…huddled against the wall behind her chair.

What should she do now?

She couldn't go out the front. Wouldn't risk going out the back. He could be watching there, too. But she had to hide somewhere before the others arrived.

Her mind whirled with confusion. One escape scenario after the other tumbled through her mind, each one less feasible than the last. She squeezed her eyes shut in the darkness and forced her thoughts to slow. She had to think clearly here. Had to have a strategy.

There was no place to hide that they wouldn't look.

A whimper escaped her brutal hold on her emotions. They were going to kill her.

The phone.

She could call for help.

She edged toward her desk once more.

The police would arrive in mere minutes.

Relief flooded her.

A scrape of boot heel on concrete echoed just outside the door.

She froze.

He would hear her.

No matter how fast the police arrived it would be too late.

She'd already be dead.

She had to hide.

Leaving her shoes behind to aid in her stealth and moving as quickly as she dared for fear of making even the slightest sound, Kelly headed toward the lounge. She knew the floor plan by heart, which prevented her from bumping into anything since Ray was a stickler for everything being in its place.

Inside the bathroom she drew the door closed behind her. It was as dark as pitch but she didn't dare turn on a light. She had to think. Had to hide.

They would likely look in the vanity cabinet which was the only place in the room she could conceal herself. There really was no safe place. Not Ray's office, not the lobby or the lounge including the bathroom, definitely not in the small conference room. Not a single room in the entire suite offered any hope whatsoever.

She was dead.

Another whimper burgeoned in her throat.

Her fingers clenched more tightly around the disk.

No.

She had to get through this.

Had to do it for Ray and Ann.

Whoever had done this, she would see that they paid. If this disk contained evidence, she couldn't let them find it. It had to be about the disk. He'd told the caller he had it, but apparently suspected there could be a copy. She stood on shaky legs and tucked the disk into the pocket of her slacks. Think, Kelly, she ordered. There had to be a way to do this.

There was a toilet, a small supply cabinet and the vanity in this room.

She looked upward. Though she couldn't see a thing, she remembered the acoustic tiles that made up the ceiling. There would be room above them but she couldn't be sure the slim framework would hold her weight. She couldn't take the risk. If she broke any- thing or knocked something down he would know someone had been here.

Where could she hide?

Dammit! There had to be a place.

The ventilation return.

She stood stock still as she considered the possi- bility. It was in the corridor. The opening was twenty by thirty inches, she knew. She'd bought the filters often enough, even changed them on occasions. Her heart started to beat faster once more, this time with anticipation. That would work. Though she couldn't escape that way since the duct would lead directly into the heating and cooling unit, she could hide.

Holding her breath, she exited the bathroom and moved noiselessly through the lounge. She listened intently for ten seconds before slipping back into the corridor. She prayed the killer was still outside.

He was supposed to be hanging around out front. He'd said he would wait. She chewed her lower lip and forced herself to think. She could sneak into Ray's office and call for help. There wasn't a phone in the lounge. But there was one in Ray's office and in the conference room.

Why hadn't she thought of that?

Stupid! Stupid!

She pressed against the wall and moved cautiously toward the conference room. Dark or not, she had no desire to go into Ray's office with…with him in there dead.

"It's about time."

The words echoed from just outside the front entrance.

The sound paralyzed her.

More voices.

It was dark outside and she couldn't see a damned thing, but she could hear.

She didn't have time to make a call.

She had to hide.

Only two small latches held the grill closed over the return duct. She turned them one at a time, then drew the grill open. Her fingers trembling she moved the filter out of the way, setting it to one side in the duct. Sliding in feet first, she settled into the duct and then pulled the grill closed. The latches were a bit harder to turn from the inside, but she managed. Just as she angled the filter back into place footsteps echoed in the lobby.

They were inside.

She'd barely made it.

The seeking glow of flashlights moved about. Low voices murmured but she couldn't make out the words. She eased as far into the long metal tunnel as she dared, putting as much distance between her and the opening as possible.

The heating unit kicked on and air from the corridor rushed over her, the roar of the unit drowning out all other sound. She made herself as small as possible and waited for the temperature in the office to reach the necessary point so that the thermostat would turn off the flow of air.

The irritating roar came three more times before the endless waiting was over. Between the blasts of climate-controlling activity, she heard the intruders rummaging through every filing cabinet, desk and supply cabinet in the entire suite that made up the financial consulting and investment firm of Raymond Jarvis. Tears stung her eyes. Ray was dead. She pushed the horror away and focused on figuring out what these awful people could be looking for. It didn't make sense. They didn't keep money here. No negotiable stocks or bonds. She simply had no idea. The whole thing was crazy. Unless…it simply was the disk in her pocket.

Had Ray done business with the wrong kind of people? She couldn't believe that. She had access to his accounts and files. If there was anything underhanded going on it was definitely well hidden. She might not have any prior experience but she knew the signs to look for. Ray was clean, she was certain of it.

She thought of the disk he'd given her and his insistence that she take it home with her.

Had he suspected something like this might happen?

The grill on the return duct suddenly opened.

Kelly's heart stuttered to a stop. Her breath evaporated in her lungs.

The filter poked inward and a pair of gloved hands

felt along the surrounding walls. She pressed her face against her arms and held her breath.

"There's nothing here."

She didn't dare lift her head until she heard footsteps retreating in the corridor. The grill door stood open, the filter bent and sticking haphazardly to one side, affording her scarcely any protection from view. But the inside of the duct was dark and so were her clothes. It wasn't likely anyone would see her unless they stuck their head in and shined a light directly on her.

Keeping her face shielded with her arms, she listened as the men, four she decided, set the office to rights. Two of them didn't like it, but one had ordered that they were to leave things as they found them. She heard the killer's voice once or twice more. It made her want to run like hell, but she couldn't move…could scarcely afford to draw a breath.

What felt like an eternity later, the intruders left by the front entrance.

For a very long time Kelly huddled there in the silence, afraid to move.

Then she started to cry.

The tears came in long, choking sobs.

When she'd regained control of her emotions, she eased out of the long, dusty tunnel. She sat on the corridor floor for a while before she tried to stand. Still emotional, Kelly felt her way along the corridor. Since the lights were still out and she didn't trust instinct to keep her from banging into something. When she reached her desk, careful to access it from the front, she snatched up the telephone and punched in 9-1-1.

Dear God.

How could this have happened?

Who were those men?

She hadn't seen their faces and couldn't identify them.

The killer's voice echoed inside her head. She did know his voice. But that's all she knew about him.

But he knew her.

He'd come here to kill her.

Thought he had.

What would he do when he learned she was still alive?

''9-1-1, what's the nature of your emergency?''

Kelly hung up the phone without saying a word.

Chapter Two

Victoria smiled as she viewed the lovely thank-you cards embossed with hers and Lucas's name.

Lucas Camp and Victoria Colby-Camp

It didn't seem possible, but her dream of sharing her life with Lucas had finally come true. She fingered the raised lettering, her heart warming at the memory of her wedding day.

The chapel had been filled to overflowing. Her loyal staff from the agency as well as numerous members of Lucas's unit of specialists had attended. Dear friends from the community here in Chicago as well as in Washington, D.C., had come to witness the moment so long in the making.

Leberman had failed. He'd tried for years to destroy her. Had been successful in murdering her husband and stealing her son. But Victoria had not given up. With Lucas's strong, loving support, she had fought Leberman and won. Her chest constricted when she thought of all that her son had endured at the evil bastard's hand. He'd abused Jim endlessly, brainwashed him and turned him into a killing machine. But, in the end, Leberman's plan had failed. For as soon as Jim realized the truth, something long-buried inside him had pushed to the surface, ultimately saving Victoria's life as well as his own. He had not been able to complete the mission for which he had been trained for most of his life: killing his own mother. That was behind them now. They had to look to the future.

Victoria had her son back, she was now married to the man she loved, and Errol Leberman was rotting in hell. Life was just as it should be.

The ceremony had been every bit as beautiful as she had dreamed it would be. She and Lucas had pledged their lives to one another. Had publicly taken the vows that their hearts had taken long ago. They'd been in love with each other for years. And somehow, as the ceremony had concluded with the minister pronouncing them husband and wife, Victoria had known that James, her first true love, had been watching. She felt his love even now, and his blessing. He would want her to be happy. He would want their son to be safe and happy.

Her son grew stronger each day. The road to recovery after such a thorough brainwashing and such horrendous abuse would be long and arduous, but James Colby, Jr., was a strong man. Plus, he had a woman who loved him at his side. Tasha North, the undercover agent who had gotten close to him before his true identity was known, had fallen deeply in love with him. Victoria suspected that the next wedding she attended would be her son's. But he had a ways to go yet. The nightmares were still an ever present part of his life and he still suffered memory lapses.

Time was all he needed.

Victoria pushed away from her desk and strolled toward the kitchen of her new home. She and Lucas had decided that a new home was in order. Her son had asked her to keep the lake house, though she wasn't quite sure why he felt the need to go there from time to time. Whatever it took to make him happy was all that mattered. She'd sold her small home in the gated community where she'd lived since her first husband's death. That home had been a place of slow healing, of coming to terms with the cruel fate she'd been dealt. She wanted her life with Lucas to begin in a new place where memories would be made, not relived.

The lovely home, only thirty minutes from her office, was not only large and sunny, it was also in the midst of a quiet neighborhood where security gates and guards weren't necessary. She no longer felt the need for such extreme measures. The devil she had feared so long was no more.

The only thing that wasn't as it should be just now was work. She'd returned to the office for a few weeks, but Lucas wasn't quite ready to share her so completely. He'd promised to take another month off after their wedding if she would. How could she turn down an offer like that? Lucas Camp taking a month off from work in addition to the time he'd already taken for their wedding? That might not happen again in this lifetime. In truth, she could use some more time with her son. They'd lost a great deal of that precious commodity, she wanted to make up for every minute and then some. She had a competent staff who could take care of things a while longer.

She found Lucas in the kitchen preparing an afternoon snack tray of fruit and cheese. The wine was already breathing on the counter. Another smile tugged the corners of her mouth upward. Who would have guessed that he would be so domesticated? It just didn't get better than this.

"Surely you haven't finished all those thank-you cards already?" Lucas teased as she joined him at the kitchen's generous island. He'd tried to talk her into allowing her secretary, Mildred, to help her with the work of responding to all the gifts they had received, but Victoria refused. She wanted to attend to each one personally, even if getting around to it had been a long time coming.

"I'm making headway," she allowed, determined not to let him know just how slowly the process was going.

"Ian called," Lucas told her.

She'd heard the phone ring but had assumed it was for Lucas. "Really?" Anticipation percolated through her. She did so miss her work. "Is everything all right at the office?" It was Saturday, the office was closed. Or it was supposed to be, unless a case had gone awry. A twinge of anxiety quickly followed the path the anticipation had taken.

A muscle in Lucas's jaw flexed once, twice, before

he answered. Not good. "Everything's fine. It's just that a new client contacted Ian when he couldn't reach either you or Mildred."

Their home had a new telephone number, one the few clients she gave her personal number to wouldn't have, and Mildred was spending the holiday weekend with her niece, Angel. With no children of her own, Mildred thought of Angel as a daughter…thought of her child as a grandchild.

Putting her reflections aside, Victoria asked, "Did Ian mention a name?" She knew Lucas was being purposely evasive. At this rate he'd never be ready for her to return to work permanently. It was more than simply his desire to be with her. He wanted to protect her, she'd suffered a great deal. But, he also fully understood how she felt. She would not allow her agency to suffer.

"Senator William Lester from Texas."

Bill? Victoria frowned. She hadn't spoken to him in years. Not since his daughter had gone missing. They'd feared kidnapping, but no ransom had come. The FBI couldn't garner any leads so Bill had come to the Colby Agency. It hadn't taken Victoria's top-notch staff long to determine that the somewhat rebellious girl had run away with dreams of becoming an actress before bothering with college. She'd come home willingly and had since turned into a fine young lady, graduating from her father's alma mater at the top of her class. She'd simply been young and gullible and hoped to spread her wings a little more than her strict father had allowed. She'd lived and learned. Luckily. Considering the young people who went missing every day and turned up dead, it could have ended very differently. Victoria knew firsthand.

"What's going on with the senator?" Victoria prodded since Lucas didn't appear compelled to fill her in.

His hands stilled in their work of arranging grapes on the tray. "We don't know." His solemn gaze met hers. "He won't talk to anyone but you."

Renewed anticipation soared through Victoria. "Well, I suppose I'd better get to the office then."

"He and Ian are on their way here."

Victoria took Lucas's hand in hers. "Thank you. I know you don't want to allow work to intrude right now. I appreciate your patience."

Lucas pulled her into his arms and her heart fluttered at the strength he emanated. "I knew what I was getting into when I married you, Victoria." He smiled, the intensity of it made her quiver with pleasure. "Your loyalty to your staff and clients is part of what I love about you. I just want to be sure it's safe for you to dive fully back into work."

She tensed ever so slightly, hoping he wouldn't notice, but, of course, he did. "Lucas, I'm aware that you still feel there are unanswered questions. I appreciate the concern, but Leberman is dead, what difference does it make how he gleaned his information about us?"

"It may not make any," Lucas conceded. "But I have to be certain. There is no margin for error when dealing with a man like Leberman."

She nodded. "I don't disagree with that assessment and I've consented to this additional leave. However," she dreaded his reaction to the next part, "eventually I'll be returning to work unless you have overwhelming evidence that persuades me to do otherwise."

"Understood," he relented, almost too easily. Did he know something already? Had he discovered some new evidence that had prompted him to insist on this additional leave? He would tell her in his own time. "Now, let's take the wine and the tray into the parlor and await our guests."

Within moments of their settling, the doorbell rang. Lucas greeted Ian and the senator and escorted them to the parlor. Victoria banished thoughts of Leberman and his evil legacy back to some rarely visited recess of her mind.

"Victoria, I apologize for the intrusion," Ian said, clearly torn between doing the right thing for the agency and following the strict orders Lucas had issued.

"It's perfectly fine, Ian."

"Victoria." The senator embraced her briefly. "It's wonderful to see you."

"You're looking well, Bill," she returned. "How's that lovely daughter of yours?"

"Getting married in June," he beamed. "Her fiancé is in politics as well."

"That's wonderful," Victoria enthused. "I'm sure you're very proud."

"Have a seat, Senator," Lucas suggested, "and I'll do the honors." He gestured to the refreshments he'd prepared.

When they were seated, Lucas served the wine. Ian,

as she had known he would, declined since, for all intents and purposes, he was on duty.

Victoria savored her wine as Lucas and Bill conversed about the current political climate in Texas as well as Washington. She could simply sit and watch her husband for hours on end. She did so love this man. But there was a time for that and it wasn't now.

"So, Senator, tell me what brings you northward." Lucas broached the matter at hand first. But then that was Lucas. He did things his way, in his own time and always one step ahead of even his sharpest peer.

The senator looked from Lucas to Victoria and back.

"You may speak freely," she said before he could say what she felt certain he was thinking. "Don't doubt the loyalties of either of these men."

Bill nodded. "Of course." He fingered the stem of his glass a moment before beginning. "I'm sure you're aware that most states have their drug issues, those that border other countries in particular."

She nodded. She was very much aware of the drug situation in Texas, especially along the border of Mexico where traffickers used the wide-open space to their advantage. It was nearly impossible to cover all those miles with any real efficiency.

The senator cleared his throat and continued. "I have reason to believe that the Texas drug cartel extends very high in the political hierarchy of the state."

Victoria lifted a skeptical brow. "How high?" Uneasiness crept over her. Whenever one politician accused another there was always a question of motivation. Bill Lester was a fine man, but he was only human.

"The governor's office."

After sipping her wine she set her glass aside. "If I recall," she said cautiously, not wanting to put him on the defensive, "this is the same governor with whom you have openly exchanged heated words in the past?" She'd put it as delicately as she could. The truth was, Senator William Lester and Governor George Vann had been at each other's throats for years. The two men openly despised each other and the whole world knew it.

"One and the same," he admitted. "But this is different. I'm trying to keep my suspicions to myself until I'm certain."

"You think the governor is enabling the cartel in some way?" Lucas tossed out. "Turning a blind eye here and there perhaps?"

"That and possibly more," Bill explained. "Now it appears the FBI may even be involved."

"In what way?" Ian wanted to know. He was a former U.S. marshal himself, and his wife had been an FBI agent for many years, so his reservations were understandable.

Bill loosened his tie. "Raymond Jarvis operated a small financial consulting and investment firm in Houston. I've known him for years. Considered him a friend. He came to me about two months ago and expressed concern regarding one of his new clients. Though neither of us could be sure if this client was connected to the cartel, we both worried that it was a major possibility. Ray was running scared. He felt certain this client was using him to launder drug money. He wanted me to help him.'' The senator looked pointedly at Victoria. ''Considering my history with the governor, whatever goes down where he is concerned needs to come from some other source. Otherwise, he'll insist that I had a hand in making him look bad. I can't risk the truth being overlooked because I was involved in bringing his wrongdoing to light. I suggested that Ray contact the FBI and go from there.''

''Did he take your advice?'' Victoria had a feeling the man had, which accounted for the senator's suspicions where the Bureau was concerned.

''About one month ago Ray told me that he was working with an agent. He seemed relieved so I left it at that. He said he'd keep me posted.'' He rubbed his forehead and released a heavy sigh. ''Last evening someone entered Ray's office and killed him, his assistant and the FBI agent who'd been working with him.''

Victoria and Ian exchanged a look.

''Do the police have any leads?'' Lucas inquired.

The senator shook his head. ''Not yet. Nothing appears to have been touched. We have no way of being certain if anything was taken since the two people who worked at the office, Ray and his assistant, were both murdered.''

''And the agent,'' Ian asked next, ''had he left any reports or evidence he'd gathered regarding Raymond Jarvis's claim? Perhaps he had discussed the case with a fellow agent.''

''That's the really strange part. There is no indication whatsoever that the agent had ever even met with Ray before. The only thing connecting him is his presence at the scene and an envelope with Ray's company logo on it. The envelope contained twenty-five thousand dollars in cash. The homicide detectives discovered it in the agent's jacket pocket. You can imagine the conclusion those in charge of the investigation have drawn.''

"Convenient," Lucas commented.

"My thinking exactly," Bill agreed.

"What do you need from the Colby Agency?'' Victoria ventured, cutting to the chase.

"I'm sure the authorities will do what they can. The Bureau is coordinating their investigation with the locals. But, considering this turn of events with the Bureau, I'm not sure I can count on the normal channels of law enforcement. I owe it to Ray to find out what happened. To do that I need the best." His gaze settled on Victoria's. "Your agency is the best. I want you to find out what went wrong. Why Ray and his assistant are dead and why an FBI agent with an outstanding record is not only dead but suspected of having taken a bribe.''

"Trent Tucker comes to mind," Victoria said to Ian. "He grew up in Texas. Used to be a bounty hunter there. I'm certain he would be the best man for the job.''

"I'll call him at home and brief him on the situation," Ian added. He turned to the senator. "We're going to need access to any resources at your disposal. Copies of the detectives' reports. Forensics assessments.''

"I can get anything you need," the senator told him. "Tell Mr. Tucker I'll provide a copy of whatever the police have on the case."

After settling on the final arrangements, Victoria and Lucas saw their visitors to the door.

"Thanks again, Victoria," Bill said solemnly. "I knew I could count on the Colby Agency for top-notch work and discretion."

Once Ian and the senator had gone, Lucas closed and locked the door behind them. He leaned against it then and allowed the weight of his gaze to rest upon Victoria.

"You promised me this additional time," he reminded.

"I did," she acquiesced.

"Fair enough."

Though she knew Lucas was only concerned for her welfare, the gravity of his last comment had felt very much like a warning. And yet she sensed it was not. He only wanted the best for her. Lucas Camp would go to any lengths to protect her.

Dread trickled through her. He had to know something to be playing out this scenario so doggedly. And whatever it was, it could not be good.

Galveston, Texas
Saturday, 4:30 p.m.

KELLY HUDDLED in the shower stall beneath the hot spray of water and still it did nothing to make her feel warm again. She kept seeing the blood soak through the white silk of Ann's blouse. Kept seeing the third eye someone had given Ray. And the man who'd been in his office—she shuddered—the whole back of his head had been blown off.

Stuff like that happened on television…to other people. Not to quiet, insignificant folks like her…like Ann and Ray. It was crazy. Didn't make sense.

Even after nearly twenty-four hours, she couldn't bring herself to turn on the television. It was as if seeing it on the news would make it more real.

She'd lain in that air duct for long minutes, maybe hours, before she'd crawled out. She'd turned on the desk lamp in Ray's office and seen more than she wanted to with that meager glow. Eventually she'd sat down next to Ann and held her cold hand. She didn't know how long she'd sat there, until she'd realized she had to go. Had to hide before they came back and found her. Before the police found her. Her hang-up on the 9-1-1 operator would eventually culminate in the police's arrival.

If anyone discovered that she was still alive, the killer would come for her.

She'd watched enough movies and read enough suspense novels to know how that went. She was a witness. She had evidence. She thought of the disk. Whoever the bad guys were they would want her dead.

She had only one option. She had to learn who the bad guys were and then take the evidence to the police. But she couldn't do anything until she was sure who the enemy was. She refused to trust even the police with her life until she knew the situation a little better.

That might make her a fool, but at least she was a living one.

Once she'd worked up the nerve and to keep up the necessary pretense, she'd taken Ann's car, the keys had been clutched in her icy fingers. Her purse had been in her car. Kelly had driven straight to Galveston and hidden out in Ann's home. She'd never been in any trouble, not even a traffic ticket—at least not until that morning. She'd forgotten to put her driver's license in her purse yesterday morning. She'd taken them out to verify a check the night before and then stuffed them into her jeans pocket. Stupidly she'd forgotten about it and had driven to work without her license. The one time in her life she'd been driving without them and she'd been pulled over. Not only did she get a ticket, but there was a hefty fine attached.

Just her luck.

Anyway, there were no prints on file, no nothing. She had no record whatsoever. She and Ann were about the same size. They had the same blond hair, just different eye colors. Ann's was more brown than hazel. Kelly's was definitely hazel. If the police thought Ann was her for just a few days maybe it would buy Kelly enough time to figure out what the hell was going on.

The water started to cool so she forced herself to get up and out of the shower. When she'd towel dried, she wrapped herself in Ann's robe and forced herself to consider eating. She hadn't eaten in more than twenty-four hours. She would need her strength if she was going to conduct this investigation. There was no

one she could call upon for help. She didn't have any
real friends to speak of, other than Ann. She shuddered. An only child, her parents had passed away
shortly after she'd graduated high school. First her
mother to cancer, then her father to grief. He hadn't
lived a year after her mother had died. He'd loved
her too much to live without her.

Kelly made a disgusted sound. If only men like that
existed anymore. Her father had been the bravest, tru-
est man she'd ever known. A cowboy through and
through. But Kelly hadn't been able to bear living on
the ranch without them. She'd leased the place and
moved to the big city to finish her education and start
a new life.

She might never find herself a cowboy to love her
the way her father had loved her mother, but she
would have the career she'd always dreamed of. Even
that possibility looked dim now.

Her whole life was down the toilet.

She opened a can of soup and poured it into a mi-
crowave safe bowl. Surely she could keep soup down.
Felix, Ann's big old calico cat, curled around her legs.
Kelly supposed Felix wanted to eat, too.

When she'd heated her soup, she put it on a tray
with a glass of milk and crackers. Then she opened
a can of cat food for Felix who purred appreciatively.

Gathering her courage around her, Kelly sat down
on the sofa and turned on the television for the first
time since all this insanity started.

She surfed until she found a channel showing the
news. While the weatherman spouted his forecast for
a warmer than average New Year's Eve, she forced

down the soup and crackers, only then realizing how hungry she was. By the time the image of Ray's office flashed on the screen, she'd managed to eat enough to sustain her. Any appetite she'd had left vanished as the reporter gravely related the events of the previous night. The numbness set in again. The man who'd been in Ray's office wasn't named, which she found odd. She wished now she'd had the nerve to look in his wallet for identification. But no way could she have done that. She'd been lucky to get out without vomiting, which would have left evidence of her survival.

She turned off the television and took her tray back to the kitchen. Working on autopilot, she cleaned up after herself and went to Ann's office.

Kelly studied the disk for a few moments before inserting it into Ann's computer. She wasn't sure what she would find, but there was no putting it off any longer.

She had to know the truth.

Starting with the disk seemed as good a first step as any.

Chapter Three

At six foot three, a first-class seat was about the only place Trent Tucker was comfortable on a commercial airliner. Not to mention it gave him a little more privacy to peruse the kind of reports he was reviewing this morning.

Heavy icing had delayed all flights departing from Chicago on Sunday so he'd had no choice but to postpone his departure until Monday morning. To bring him up to speed and to prevent further delay, Senator William Lester had kindly faxed him the reports and photos pertinent to the Jarvis case last evening.

The images in the photos were gruesome. Three murders. Each victim cut down in the midst of going about his or her business. What Trent needed to know was had that business been the motivation for murder? Were three people dead because Raymond Jarvis had gotten in bed with the wrong folks? And was

twenty-five thousand dollars enough to buy an FBI
agent with an otherwise spotless record? Or was it
merely a fraction of the full payment? What about the
assistant? Was she involved or had she simply been
at the wrong place at the wrong time?

Trent shuffled the pages until he came to the data
sheet on Jarvis's assistant. Kelly Pruitt would turn
twenty-three her next birthday. She had no close family and had graduated from a Texas university at the
top of her class. She had no criminal record and a
perfect credit score. The money she'd inherited when
her parents had died had seen her through college and
then some. She had a handsome savings and a healthy
balance in checking. Midsize and modest summed up
her taste in automobiles. Her living space appeared a
bit more luxurious, judging by the address. She just
didn't fit the profile of someone looking to get involved in criminal activity.

The next data sheet detailed the life of her forty-
eight-year-old boss. Unlike Kelly, Ray Jarvis had
scraped by in college, making the necessary grades
by the skin of his teeth. He'd first gone into business
with a partner who later became his wife. Unfortunately, fourteen years and two children down the
road, the two divorced and dissolved the partnership,
which was on the brink of bankruptcy. Jarvis, however, had learned a few things. Picking up the pieces
of his life he'd started his own business and thrived.
Ten years after that he was on the verge of becoming
a major player in the financial world of the Lone Star
state.

Jarvis had worked hard to get to where he was, it

didn't make sense to Trent that he'd get greedy at this point and risk everything. But then, he wouldn't be the first guy who had turned stupid as he neared fifty. A midlife crisis took its toll on many.

The FBI agent, Norton Davis, seemed an even less likely candidate for duplicity. Thirty-one, a wife and new baby, the man had a stellar record. He had been third generation law enforcement and a pillar of the small community where he and his family resided just minutes outside Dallas.

None of it made sense. And yet, three people were dead and dirty money had changed hands.

A gasp startled Trent back to the present.

"I'm...I'm sorry," the flight attendant said. Her eyes were wide as her gaze went from the photos spread on the tray in front of him to his. "I...thought you might like some more coffee."

Trent shuffled the photos and reports into a file folder and smiled up at the nervous woman. "No thank you, ma'am."

She managed a shaky smile. "You must be the detective."

"That's right." He didn't bother with the distinction of *private* detective. She was already nervous enough. Of course, seeing photos of a homicide scene would do that. But she would know a detective was onboard since he'd checked his weapon, which was packed and secured for the flight along with his one piece of luggage.

The stewardess nodded and continued down the aisle, her posture a little stilted.

Trent glanced at his watch. He had another thirty

minutes before arriving in Houston. Plenty of time to further analyze the data he'd reviewed. Immediately his thoughts went to Kelly Pruitt. His gut told him that she was the true victim here. He doubted she had known what she was getting into. Jarvis, if he had gotten involved with the drug cartel, had brought this on himself. Agent Davis knew the risks and hazards of his job. But Kelly Pruitt was just a kid…she'd had no idea that death lurked so close.

At thirty-three, Trent was old enough to know that youth didn't necessarily equate to innocence, but he had a feeling about this young woman. He leaned back in his seat and stretched out his long legs as best he could. If she proved as innocent as he suspected, he would make this right for that little lady. Whoever had murdered her wouldn't get away with it. He'd spent six years as a bounty hunter in the great state of Texas. Sniffing out and bringing in his quarry was what he did best. Patience and persistence always paid off in that line of work and there wasn't a more patient or a more determined man on the planet.

"YOU MUST BE Mr. Tucker," a man suggested as Trent exited the gate at Houston's Hobby Airport. "Detective Hargrove." He extended his hand. Houston's police department would be working aspects of this case along with the FBI—because the senator didn't trust the local Bureau.

It hadn't been necessary for the detective to introduce himself. Trent recognized the cop instantly. Wrinkled suit, probably hadn't been home all weekend, and a five o'clock shadow well before noon. If he was the detective in charge of this case, Trent doubted he'd get any rest before it was solved. With a senator breathing down his neck he likely wouldn't even sleep until he had a suspect. He looked to be about forty. Fairly trim, but with a haggard expression that lent credence to Trent's conclusion.

Which, considering what they had to go on, wasn't happening anytime soon. This was one of those dig in for the long haul kind of cases. Trent could feel it all the way to his bones. There would be no clear-cut answers. No handy suspects. This one would be solved one tidbit of revealed evidence at a time. Slowly and methodically.

The idea didn't intimidate Trent in the least. Waiting out his prey was something he did especially well.

Trent shook the other man's outstretched hand. "I appreciate you coming out to meet me like this considering it's a holiday," Trent offered.

Hargrove rolled his bloodshot eyes. "What holiday? Until I catch the perp in this case I doubt I'll even see my family again."

Trent had been right. "I understand."

"You want to go to the scene first, right?"

"Right."

After a trip to luggage pickup, Hargrove led the way to the short-term parking area where two dark sedans waited. He gestured to one and offered Trent a set of keys. "I figured the least we could do was provide you with transportation seeing how you're going to be cooperating with us and all."

Trent accepted the keys. "Sounds fair to me." He tossed his luggage in the back seat and settled behind the wheel. The Houston Police Department didn't want him uncovering anything without keeping them fully informed. He imagined there would be a tracking device somewhere on the sedate-looking vehicle just so they would know where he was at all times. No one wanted this case to go any farther south than it already was. And no one, not H.P.D. or the senator, wanted the Bureau to know Trent was involved.

Forty-five minutes after leaving the airport, Hargrove turned into a small parking area that supported a minioffice complex on the fringes of Houston proper. Three separate suites made up the complex with Jarvis's on the end. An overgrown jungle of shrubbery camouflaged the aging building from its newer two-story neighbor.

Yellow crime-scene tape and a posted warning at the entrance marked the area as off-limits to anyone but official personnel. To breach that line was a criminal offense.

Hargrove unlocked the door and entered the premises. Trent took his time as he moved inside, studying the layout and looking for anything that appeared out of place. The lobby was relatively small, tiled floor, upholstered chairs and a couple of tables covered with magazines for waiting clients. The assistant's desk stood on the far side of the room where the space narrowed into a corridor that led to the other offices, he surmised.

The assistant's desk was tidy. A small green plant occupied one corner. A chalk outline on the floor behind it represented the young woman who had been murdered there.

"Her purse was taken as evidence," Hargrove told him, noting the path of Trent's gaze. "There wasn't much in it though. A few dollars, a credit card, sunglasses, and lip gloss and tissues."

Without looking up from the outline, Trent asked, "No driver's license or other ID?"

"Apparently she left home without her license that morning, even got a ticket on the way to work. Oh." The detective shook his head. "Forgot to mention that, the ticket was in her purse as well."

Trent nodded.

"Look around all you'd like," Hargrove said as he handed him a pair of latex gloves. "Jarvis's office, a lounge and a conference room are that way." He gestured to the corridor. "I'm going to make some calls."

Hargrove took a seat in the lobby and fished out his cell phone. Trent, thankful for the opportunity to view the rest of the scene alone, tugged on the gloves and entered Jarvis's office first. He preferred making his own assessments, with no outside influence.

The leather executive chair behind the desk carried the mark of a single bullet hole and the dried remains of a good deal of blood. Some of the life-giving fluid had dripped onto the beige carpet. One of the upholstered chairs in front of the desk was overturned. The agent had likely stood and faced the shooter after Jarvis took a bullet. That would explain the overturned chair and the spray of blood and brain matter on Jarvis's desk. According to the M.E.'s preliminary report, the bullet had entered his forehead, leaving a small round hole, but had exited the back of his head removing a wide swath of all in its path.

Again, an outline on the floor marked the place the agent had fallen. Trent shook his head. He never doubted his first impressions and this had the look and smell of a setup.

The shooter hadn't simply walked in at just the right time to take out all involved. He had known when the agent would be arriving. Had known when the other offices would be closed, allowing additional privacy. These killings had been planned down to the precise moment—after the envelope of money was in the agent's pocket. Almost too precise.

Trent took his time going through the office, then the lounge and conference room. Everything was just as it should be. Not a single thing looked out of place.

When he returned to the corridor, he walked the full length of it. Checked the rear emergency exit, which led into an alley that backed up to a small strip mall. He moved slowly back up the corridor but stopped midway. Something snagged his attention. The grill on the return duct wasn't fully closed.

He crouched down and found one latch loose, the louvered grill that served as a door was held closed at the top only. "Hargrove!" he called.

The detective appeared pretty damned quick for a guy running on forty-eight hours or more with no sleep. "Yeah?"

"Got a flashlight?"

"In the car. I'll get it."

Trent released the one latch and pulled the grill open. The battered filter lay discarded to the side. He leaned forward and looked around inside but couldn't see anything. Why would the filter be in that condition and moved to the side? He pulled the filter from the duct and looked it over before setting it aside.

"Here you go." Hargrove came up behind him with a black, heavy-duty police issue flashlight in hand.

"Thanks." Trent surveyed the inside of the duct. About ten feet long. Not much to see other than the thin layer of insulation coating the sheet metal. As far as he could tell it was undisturbed. But when he drew back something snagged his attention.

A couple of strands of hair. He reached for it. Pulled it loose from the grill and studied it. Blond. Fairly long.

"Whatcha got there?" Hargrove squatted down next to him. "You think the unit sucked those in from the floor or whatever?"

Trent shook his head. "I don't think so. These two hairs were snagged on this metal edge where the grill frame fits into the duct." He pointed to the spot where he'd pulled them loose. "I think they got caught there when someone stuck their head in here."

"To change the filter maybe?" Hargrove suggested.

Trent shrugged. "Maybe."

But whoever had changed the filter last hadn't done a very good job, he didn't bother to mention.

"You wanna go over to the morgue now?"

"Yeah." Leaving the grill open, he stood. "I think I've seen all I need to here." His gaze settled on the detective's. "You got an evidence bag?"

"Sure." Hargrove pulled a plastic bag from his jacket pocket and bagged the hair. "You want me to put it with the rest of the stuff forensics is going over?"

"Why not?"

DETECTIVE HARGROVE was a team player. Trent was glad for that. He wasn't grandstanding and didn't mind outside interference. Trent felt damn lucky. It rarely worked that way. Most cops didn't like P.I.'s horning in on their cases. But then, he supposed, any sort of help would be a relief considering the way the senator was pulling rank.

The morgue was like all others. Cold, clinical and smelling of chilled flesh. Focusing on the task rather than the environment, Trent considered the bodies one by one. Jarvis and the FBI agent were pretty much what he had expected. The assistant, however, was not.

Trent walked all the way around the extended drawer and considered the victim from both sides. She looked older than twenty-two. A little tall for the description on her license as well. And the shape of the face wasn't quite right.

"Has anyone identified the body?" Trent asked the detective who hovered a few feet away.

"Not yet. There's no family other than a distant cousin who lives in Massachusetts. She's flying in tomorrow to claim the body."

Trent had a feeling she was going to be startled. "Did you print her or verify her identity with her dental records?"

The detective shrugged. "We haven't got a response back yet on the request we put out for dental records and she doesn't have any kind of record so she's not in the fingerprint database. Printing her seemed pointless."

When little was known about the victim and there was no family left behind to provide information, a request was sent to local dentists and physicians to see if the victim was one of their patients. But a response took time.

Trent surveyed the body again, his gaze going back to the eyes. "Contacts?" He nodded toward her eyes.

"Not according to the M.E.'s preliminary report. Full autopsies weren't necessary since the cause and manner of death was obvious but he would have listed contact lenses in the abbreviated autopsy reports."

Trent studied the color a bit closer. "Then why are her eyes brown when her driver's license says she has hazel eyes?" His gaze shifted to the detective who didn't bother to ask how Trent had gotten a look at her license. When he'd been a bounty hunter in Texas he'd had his sources. He'd wasted no time yesterday getting a copy of each victim's driver's license so he'd have a clean visual.

A frown had marred across Hargrove's forehead. "I don't know." His gaze collided with Trent's. "Are you suggesting that she isn't Kelly Pruitt?"

Trent considered the body again, his gut clenching in anticipation. "Run her prints just in case." She had similar blond hair to that of the image in Kelly Pruitt's license photo as well as the hairs he'd collected from the grill over the duct at the office. "You might want to compare her hair with those we found, though it might not be relevant since the hair could be left over from a previous assistant.''

Hargrove swore. ''The last assistant Jarvis employed was a brunette. I've already questioned her. If this woman isn't Kelly Pruitt and we didn't discover that fact until now, there's going to be hell to pay.'' He swore again. ''And there was that 9-1-1 hang-up. We thought maybe she tried to call before she collapsed.''

Trent understood completely. He wouldn't want to be in the detective's shoes because he had a bad feeling that this body belonged to someone else.

If his instincts were on the mark, Kelly Pruitt was still alive. Out there. Somewhere.

The only question was whether she was hiding from the killer or abetting him.

KELLY'S EYES OPENED and she groaned.

The pages she'd printed out were plastered to her face, she realized with another groan. She raised up from the desk, peeling away the research she'd worked on until dawn. Felix the cat stretched and made a languid sound before leaping from the desktop and scurrying from the room. At least one of them had gotten some real sleep last night.

Her shoulders ached and her head throbbed dully. She should have stopped and gone to bed hours ago. Swiping a hand over her face, she sighed. But then sleeping would have allowed her to dream and she just hadn't been ready to face those haunting nightmares again. The images from Friday evening poured one over the other into her mind. She banished them instantly and forced her cramped legs to hold up her weight as she pushed out of her chair.

She couldn't say much for falling asleep at the computer, but at least the night had passed without her having to relive those horrors yet again.

She staggered to the bathroom and turned on the shower. The disk Ray had insisted she take home with her had revealed nothing as of yet. Access required a codeword. Hours of guesswork had not revealed the proper nine-letter word. She'd tried combinations of letters and numbers with no luck there, either. Whatever was on the file she couldn't access it. Yet. She had no intention of giving up.

Her clothes left in a pile on the floor, she stepped into the shower and let the hot water sluice over her tired muscles. It felt like heaven after a long stretch in hell. Frustration at not being able to access the disk had sent her on another mission. She'd perused Ann's inbox as a means of distraction. Her friend hadn't received any new e-mails since last Thursday, which surprised Kelly just a little. The only interesting part of her exploration was the numerous cyber love letters from Romeo.

Kelly shivered when she thought of the man's sexy style of delivery. He took even the most innocuous of comments to a whole new level. No wonder Ann had been enamored with him. She'd told Kelly she had herself an online romance going. Things had definitely been heating up. Though the two, apparently, had not shared actual personal data. Romeo had not revealed his real name, address or profession and, as far as Kelly knew, Ann hadn't, either.

Of course, that was the safe way to handle the situation, but what was the point? Though Kelly had to admit that she found his e-mails titillating, how could they compare to the real thing? She washed her hair and lathered her body, her too vivid imagination conjuring the feel of strong arms and a hard male body. Unfortunately that couldn't be faked in cyberspace.

After a quick rinse and toweling off, Kelly scrubbed the residue from the steam-fogged mirror and stared at her reflection. How in the world was she going to get her life back? Would the police listen if she simply came forward and announced that she was still alive and told them the truth about what really happened?

Or would a move like that simply get her killed?

She thought of the data she'd downloaded and printed from Ray's files. Since he worked from home and the road quite often, he'd set himself up a way to access his files remotely. He'd given the code to Kelly last month when he'd had to go out of town for his last remaining aunt's funeral. She supposed even a workaholic like Ray didn't want to pull out his laptop at a funeral.

Kelly had studied the files and determined the ones as most likely candidates for money-laundering. Overseas accounts with diverse investments. Not a single one jumped out at her. Every entry to the records appeared as it should be. She didn't recognize the names on the accounts, all were corporations— another red flag when looking for trouble spots.

Whenever an individual or group of individuals wanted to dilute a situation, they formed a "dummy" corporation and invested widely. These sorts of transactions were the most difficult to monitor.

But there were other ways that could slip under the radar of anyone looking for questionable activities.

Kelly knew most of the individual account holders. She'd met them or at least spoken on the phone with them. But being polite and cordial didn't make them innocent. There was simply no way for her to know who could be trusted and who couldn't. Whatever the case, someone Ray had come into contact with had grown dissatisfied with his work and had decided his services were no longer needed. Either that or Ray had figured out that a client he represented was not what he seemed and that knowledge had proved fatal.

She turned up the volume on the television as she padded through the living room. Keeping tabs on the investigation was necessary, she reminded herself as she rummaged through Ann's kitchen in search of something to eat. Her appetite was still AWOL but eating was essential to survival.

The news anchor's voice snared her attention with one simple statement: "Now, for an update on the multiple homicide at a Houston investment firm."

Kelly dismissed thoughts of food and hurried to the living room to watch the report. She settled on the sofa as a reporter standing in front of Ray's office filled the screen. She could see the yellow crime-scene tape fluttering in the breeze where it was strung across the front entrance. Her gut clenched with dread.

Ray was dead.

Ann was dead.

"The Houston Police Department," the reporter droned solemnly, "has just released the name of the third victim in the still unsolved multiple homicide. Special Agent Norton Davis of the Dallas Federal Bureau of Investigations was murdered in the private office of Raymond Jarvis. We don't know yet whether Agent Davis was a client of Jarvis's or conducting an investigation into the firm's activities, both seem unlikely given the geography and jurisdiction. However, sources close to the investigations say—"

Kelly muted the sound and sat in stunned silence for a long while. *An FBI agent.* No wonder Ray had been nervous. She blinked. She should have gone to the police already. Should have told them what she knew.

But then news that she had survived would leak to the press.

Her gaze focused on the crime-scene tape flailing behind the reporter. If the killer hadn't hesitated to kill an FBI agent, what hope did she have of surviving once he realized his mistake?

None.

Chapter Four

Kelly Pruitt's Ashford Court residence was a two-story town house in a relatively nice neighborhood and a comfortable drive from her office.

The grounds were well landscaped, with a pool and virtual playground for adult activities such as tennis and volleyball. Her town house was a one-bedroom that overlooked the closed-for-the-winter pool and courtyard.

Inside, Detective Hargrove stood aside and allowed Trent to take his time perusing the place. The living room, dining room and kitchen made up the downstairs portion of the town house. Kelly Pruitt displayed an enormous amount of photographs, her and her parents, Trent presumed. He wondered again why no one had noticed that the dead woman couldn't be Kelly Pruitt. If there had been any question, there should have been none after setting foot in this house. Sure, the resemblance was there, but the two women were far from identical. They could pass for sisters, that was true enough. However, since he didn't want to alienate H.P.D., Trent kept his thoughts to himself.

As he sifted through bookcases and drawers, Trent found a couple of packs of recently developed photographs. When he shuffled through the snapshots he hit pay dirt.

"Here's the blonde you have in the morgue," Trent said, pointing to the woman standing next to Kelly in the photograph. It was a rather blunt statement but there really was no nice way to put it. H.P.D. had made a monumental mistake.

Hargrove came up beside him and took a good look. "Damn," he muttered.

Trent shook his head as much in sympathy for the guy as in disbelief of the oversight. "Man, I can't understand why you didn't notice the mistaken identity when faced with all these photos." He gestured to the framed images lovingly placed about the room. "The dead woman is not Kelly Pruitt. You'd have to be blind not to see it. Even in her driver's license photo, had you bothered to pull it up, the differences were easy to see." Maybe he should have kept that last remark to himself, but this bordered the ridiculous.

Hargrove stared at the floor a moment then huffed out a breath before meeting Trent's questioning gaze. "The truth is, I hadn't even been here until now. The feds wanted first look. Kelly Pruitt, they insisted, was inconsequential as far as the investigation went." He shrugged. "Hell, I was just doing what I was told. We'd have learned the mistake anyway when her next-of-kin ID'd the body or from dental records, assuming we get a hit. The brass wants this investigation to focus on Jarvis and the fed. They don't care about the assistant.''

Trent could see that happening. Kelly Pruitt, a mere assistant who likely knew nothing, wouldn't matter. The immediate focus would be on the major players and clearing up any possible wrongdoing by the Bureau—especially if it was connected to Texas politics—before the media turned the case into a circus act. The senator had been right to worry that parts of this case would be swept under the rug.

''I've spent every waking moment trying to figure out what the hell Jarvis was up to and why that fed was in his office taking a bribe.''

Trent pointed to the other woman in the photo, the real Kelly Pruitt. ''She might be able to tell us what we need to know.''

The detective nodded. ''Maybe. But whether she's involved in whatever the hell went down at that office or whether she's just scared, she's going to be hard as hell to find,'' Hargrove said wearily.

Trent turned over a few of the pictures, one by one, and read the notes jotted on the back. *At the Beach with Ann. On the* Princess Ann. This photo had clearly been taken aboard a rather large sailboat. *Thanksgiving with Ann.* In this photo Trent recognized the kitchen as the one in this town house. He would find out who this Ann was and then he'd find Kelly Pruitt.

''You keep your department off my back and keep me updated on what the feds are doing and I'll find your missing assistant,'' Trent assured him. ''I'm very good at finding people who don't want to be found.''

Hargrove nodded. "I checked you out. You used to be a bounty hunter, right?''

Trent smiled. "That's right. What we have to remember is that guilty or innocent, our girl's on the run. But she'll make the same mistake they all do. Eventually she'll go back to what she knows—to what feels safe and I'll be waiting.''

"Deal," Hargrove put in quickly. "You keep me in the loop and I'll cover your ass with the brass.''

Trent knew the man was telling the truth. A mistake like this could cost him big time. He wouldn't want anyone else to know he'd screwed up. But Trent had a sneaking suspicion that someone didn't want him to uncover this mix-up.

Hargrove's cell phone rang and Trent took the opportunity while the detective was distracted to check out the second floor. This level consisted of a large bedroom and bathroom and a sitting area that Ms. Pruitt had turned into a workout area/office. Her desk and computer stood in one corner while a treadmill occupied the other. The computer didn't reveal much. He checked the last twenty or so sites she'd visited and found that she'd been reading up on boating and studying Spanish. He wondered if she was planning a vacation or a new life. Her e-mail box was empty.

It was the bedroom that Trent found the most telling about his prey. The bed was wide and inviting, the covers exotic colors, the fabric silky. The top drawer of her dresser revealed the same slinky fabric and vivid colors in the way of undergarments. On the wall next to her bed hung a massive framed print of a cowboy sitting astride a regal black horse. The hat he wore concealed most of his face, but his identity wasn't the point. It was the quintessential image of the rugged cowboy overlooking the Texas desert. Beneath that stood an honest to God leather saddle mounted on a heavy mahogany pedestal.

The image of Kelly Pruitt sitting astride that elegant saddle wearing nothing but those naughty underthings he'd seen in her drawer immediately flashed through Trent's mind. He shook off the picture and the accompanying sensations it evoked.

Kelly Pruitt had herself a cowboy fetish. He filed that tidbit away for possible later use. French doors led to the en suite bath where a huge whirlpool-tub-for-two held center stage. The vague scent of bath oil, something flowery and feminine, still lingered in the air.

"That call was from the lab," Hargrove said as he entered the room. He let go a long, low whistle. "The lady likes cowboys I see." He looked about the bedroom noting the obvious. "That might just rule out her involvement with Jarvis." Hargrove snickered. "The guy was about as far from cowboy material as we make 'em in Texas."

Not to mention, Trent kept to himself, that Jarvis had himself a girlfriend who'd recently cut a trail back home to New Orleans. The same day he ended up dead, as a matter of fact. Just another lead that needed to be checked out. Hargrove's department was looking into that avenue, as well, but without the same fervor Trent felt. The lady hadn't cut and run without motivation. Ray Jarvis had been her bread and butter from what Trent had ascertained so far.

"Did the lab have results on the victim's prints already?" Trent hadn't expected to hear anything this quickly.

Hargrove shoved a hand through his hair. "Got a match right off the bat. One Annie Sutton. She was busted for possession with intent to sell seven years ago. Cocaine."

Trent tugged one of the photographs from his shirt pocket and looked at the woman with Kelly Pruitt. She didn't look like a junkie or a dealer for that matter. A lot could change in seven years, but then again, considering the possible reason for her murder, she may simply have moved on to more lucrative projects. The kind that afforded a person luxuries like a boat named the *Princess Ann.* He had no intention of waiting for the locals to come up with a profile on Annie Sutton, the Colby Agency could move a lot faster.

Houston P.D. was like any other big city police department with hundreds of cases to work—things took time. Colby Agency Investigator Heath Murphy was Trent's backup on this case. He could focus solely on whatever Trent needed. All it would take was one phone call, which he would make after he and Hargrove had parted company. He didn't want the detective to think he didn't trust him to do his job.

"Hello, Annie," Trent murmured as he studied her image a moment longer. He needed to know all her secrets.

When Hargrove had headed back to his precinct, Trent did two things: a quick sweep of the rental car for electronic devices—he found none—and a stop at a small diner to have some lunch. While he waited for the waitress to deliver his order, he put a call through to the agency and Heath. He also made a mental note to pick up another rental, a truck maybe.

"Three things," Trent advised Heath. "Get me a list of outgoing and incoming calls on this number." He rattled off Kelly Pruitt's home telephone number. "I'll need the addresses to go along with the numbers. See what you can find on a Darlene Whitehead. She was Jarvis's girlfriend. Lived with him for the past year, but she's nowhere to be found now. H.P.D. is trying to track her down in New Orleans. She's supposed to have family there."

"Anything else?" Heath wanted to know.

Trent couldn't help thinking that as new as Heath Murphy was to the agency, he was damn good at his job. He'd grown up in the mountains of Tennessee and was a former cop. He had good instincts and was relentless in his pursuit of details. Exactly what Trent needed right now.

"See what you can dig up on an Annie Sutton. Busted in Texas for possession and sale of coke about seven years ago. I'd like to know if she has any other aliases."

"Gotcha."

"And let Ian know that the senator and I are staying in touch," Trent added as an afterthought. Ian wanted to be sure that Trent kept the senator informed. He was an old friend of Victoria's. He was part of the heat H.P.D. was feeling just now.

Trent ended the call just as the waitress arrived with his Texas-style chili. He'd been gone from Texas for years now, but he still missed the chili. As he consumed the hearty stew he considered Kelly Pruitt and her affinity for cowboys. He hadn't played that part in a while but he had no qualms about donning the boots and hat if it got him close to the lady.

But first he had to find her.

BY DUSK on Monday night Kelly felt exhausted and utterly frustrated. Nothing in Ray's files looked questionable. Not a single item was without proper documentation.

Massaging her forehead with her fingertips she considered the only questionable thing she had inadvertently stumbled across. For some reason Ann had direct access to several of Ray's files. All four were related to the same corporation, but nowhere could Kelly find a connection between the corporation and Ann. It just didn't make sense. Why would she have had the kind of access even Kelly didn't have and she was Ray's assistant, soon to be junior partner?

It was wrong, wrong, wrong.

There was no way around the bottom line. Kelly leaned back in her chair and let go a mighty breath. She needed help. She couldn't figure this out alone.

But if she went to the police could they protect her from the killer?

She'd watched plenty of movies where witnesses were supposed to be protected but something always went wrong. Still, that didn't mean it would be that way in her situation. Maybe she was blowing this completely out of proportion.

Pushing to her feet, she decided there was no way to blow death out of proportion. Ray was dead. Ann was dead. And so was that FBI agent. If he couldn't protect himself—if the whole Bureau couldn't protect one of their own—what hope was there for an insignificant bystander like her?

She paced the small office and considered the facts as she knew them again. To her knowledge Ann and Ray hardly knew each other. She'd introduced them and they exchanged pleasantries whenever Ann dropped by her office, but that was it. Ann had never mentioned Ray in any capacity. She never asked questions about the firm or Ray or anything at all related to Kelly's work. In fact, she preferred that Kelly meet her in town. Just one more thing that made Friday evening unusual. Ann didn't, as a rule, care to come all the way across town to meet Kelly at the office. Tears burned at the back of her throat. God, she wished her friend hadn't this time.

Forcing away that last, painful thought, Kelly went back to the computer and logged on. Maybe she'd inadvertently gone into the files under her own account or Ray's. It had to be a mistake. Ann couldn't possibly have access from her home computer. Careful to stay in Ann's desktop owner account, Kelly clicked on the Internet access icon and typed in the address for Ray's firm. She selected the view files option and…the user name and password loaded into the necessary boxes instantly giving her unreserved access.

This was nuts!

She logged off and walked away from the computer. God, she needed a break. She'd been locked up in here for three days now. Cabin fever, frustration and no small measure of fear were eating away at her. Though she was pretty sure no one in this neighborhood would know her, she didn't dare stick her head out the door much less go for a walk.

She'd been to Ann's place a few times but probably not enough to be recognized by anyone. She'd certainly never been introduced to any of her friend's neighbors. Ann usually came to her house. Since she worked in downtown Houston it was simply easier that way. Or they went out of town. Ann loved the water, even owned a beautiful sailboat named the *Princess Ann.* She and Kelly had spent endless weekends on the water.

Kelly suddenly stopped in the middle of the room. She surveyed the paneled study that served as her friend's office. This two-bedroom Galveston condo had to have set her back a tidy sum. The boat was a pricey luxury, and even the car she drove was a high-end foreign job that screamed money. Ann had told her she was alone in the world, too. That was one of the things that had drawn them together, both were orphans. Ann worked as a systems analyst for a major computer corporation.

But what did she really know about her dear friend?

Did systems analysts really make that kind of money?

Or had Ann inherited big bucks from her family? She'd never mentioned her family having had money.

Kelly chewed her lower lip as she studied the filing cabinet near the desk. She could take a look. What did it matter now? Ann was dead. The burn of tears stung her eyes yet again despite the certainty that she had cried herself out the night before…or thought she had.

Feeling like the scum of the earth, Kelly made herself look at the possibility—she dug into Ann's personal files.

Nearly an hour later and after having searched the entire condo she had found nothing. She stood in the two-story entry hall and looked around her.

Not a birth certificate.

Not a bank statement.

Not even a credit card statement.

A chill crept over her. That wasn't normal.

Though the condo was expensively decorated and furnished and the closet was lined with tasteful designer clothing and the jewelry chest stood filled to overflowing, there wasn't the first personal document in the condo. Not the first photo, other than the ones Kelly had given her. No family photo albums. No keepsakes of any sort. No letters from friends or family.

Nothing that told the story of who Ann Jones was or where she had come from.

Anxiety started to knot in Kelly's gut.

Maybe it wasn't Ray who was involved with the

wrong people. Maybe it was Ann. Maybe that killer had come there for her. Kelly trembled and she hugged her arms around her middle in an effort to slow the shaking. That would explain why nothing about Ray's files looked off. It had nothing to do with Ray. But what about the FBI agent? Did they suspect Ann of some wrongdoing?

Kelly shook her head.

That just didn't make sense. Ray and Ann scarcely knew each other. Why would an FBI agent come to see Ray about Ann? But she'd had access to his files.

Kelly scrubbed her hands over her face and through her hair. She just didn't know. All she had was questions and no answers. The deeper she dug the more questions she found. But she had to remember the killer's words. He'd come there to kill Ray and his assistant. Ann's death was a mistake.

Felix meowed, making her jump.

"Sheesh!" She forced her pounding heart back down to a normal rate.

The cat curled around her legs and then strolled to the front door. He needed to go out.

Kelly moved to the door and reached for the locks. She'd been here three days and hadn't opened the door. What if she did now and someone saw her?

Felix squalled again.

She peered down at him. He must have tired of his litter box in the garage. It probably needed to be changed. She'd have to take care of that. Then again, maybe she wasn't the only one with cabin fever. He could simply want out.

Bracing herself for the worst, she flipped the dead

bolt, dragged the chain from its catch and turned the button on the knob to release the final lock. She held her breath as she opened the door just barely wide enough for Felix to slither out. As soon as he was through the door, she shut it and battened it down once more. Instantly worry plagued her as to whether the cat would return. What if he got lost? What if he never came back?

She shoved the ridiculous thoughts away. Ann let the cat go out alone. She'd seen her do it. Kelly didn't know much about cats or dogs. Her mother had suffered with numerous allergies, hairy pets being one of her worst triggers. So Kelly had grown up with nothing more than a goldfish to attend to. She had no experience with four-legged critters.

She had no experience with any of this!

Kelly tugged at her blouse. Ann's style ran a little more risqué than hers. Despite being fond of sexy undergarments, Kelly generally preferred conservative outer apparel. But without any of her own clothes, she had to borrow Ann's. The jeans were snug and a tad long, the pullover sweater tight and short, but otherwise the fit was okay. Beggars couldn't be choosers, she supposed.

Besides, she'd always been welcome to anything her friend had. Ann had always made her feel completely at home.

Friend.

That term suddenly felt like a misnomer. Kelly folded her arms over her chest and considered again what she actually knew about her friend.

They'd met right after Kelly went to work for Ray.

In a coffee shop in the mall. Kelly had decided she needed to update her wardrobe for her new job. She and Ann had hit it off right away. They'd been practically inseparable ever since, spending most weekends together. Like Kelly, Ann hadn't appeared to have much of a social life. Her only romantic interest to Kelly's knowledge was her online Romeo.

Kelly sighed. She needed to put all these questions out of her mind for a while. Tomorrow, after she'd had time to fully absorb the implications of her latest discovery she could analyze it more. Right now she just wanted to tune it all out. To distract herself.

The low hum of the television drew her gaze toward the living room. That appeared about her only option. Definitely the safest. She'd simply have to steer clear of the news channels for tonight. Just for a little while. To clear her head. To get a better grip on her composure.

Even fugitives needed a break.

She shivered at the thought.

But that's what she was.

A scratch and a lonesome yawl from Felix echoed through the closed door.

Kelly rolled her eyes. Well, it hadn't taken him long to decide he wanted back in the house. It wasn't that cold outside. Forty-five degrees maybe.

She padded to the door and reached for the lock.

Spoiled cat. He was probably hungry again, too.

A firm knock on the door sent her stumbling back two steps.

Her heart launched into her throat. The breath evaporated in her lungs.

For a split second she considered that perhaps she had imagined the sound.

The cat surely couldn't have made it.

The second knock confirmed her worst fear.

Someone was at the door.

Absolute terror paralyzed her.

What if it was the police?

Or the…

Killer?

Chapter Five

Scarcely breathing, Kelly moved toward the window in hopes of getting a glimpse of whoever was knocking on the door. The firm rap echoed a third time, making her jump yet again though she'd known the sound was coming. Once at the window she leaned in close to the wall and lifted the edge of the curtain just enough in an attempt to see outside.

Dammit.

It was too dark for her to make out anything. Why hadn't she turned on the porch light when she'd let the cat out before? Speaking of Felix, he meowed long and loud, probably wrapping around the legs of the person waiting patiently for an answer. What the hell did she do now? Sit tight and hope he or she would go away? Fear shimmered through her at the idea that the individual knocking at the door could be a burglar who'd been casing the place for days, believing the owner to be out of town.

She couldn't see the street or whatever kind of vehicle her unwanted visitor had arrived in. There was just no way to even hazard a guess. It could be a neighbor wanting to borrow a cup of sugar or something.

The telephone rang. The annoying buzz reaching the entry hall from the living room. She'd been here three days and nights and the phone hadn't rung once. Certainly no one had come to the door. And now it was Grand Central station.

Moving with the same caution as before she eased down the hall and into the living room just as the fourth ring vibrated the tension-filled air. The answering machine picked up, the sound of Ann's voice stalling Kelly in her tracks halfway across the room.

"You obviously have my number now say something interesting."

Kelly's heart started to pound even harder and a sheen of tears blurred her vision. Ann was dead. What was she doing in her home hiding out like this? Ann deserved better than to lie in some morgue unidentified.

Her resolve solidified, Kelly squared her shoulders and turned toward the entry hall once more. She might as well face the music right now, starting with whoever was at the door.

"Juliet…are you there?"

The deep masculine voice tugged her attention back to the phone.

"It's Romeo. We had a date for tonight, remember?"

The sound shivered over her skin, scraping across nerve endings already raw with emotion.

Romeo.

Ann's online boyfriend. Only he called her Juliet.

Had they set up a date to finally meet?

"I guess you changed your mind… I'll try to…"

Before he could finish the hesitant statement Kelly lunged for the phone, snatching up the receiver. "Don't hang up," she pleaded breathlessly. It wasn't until she held the receiver clutched in both hands and the words had already slipped past her lips that realization slammed into her brain. What the hell was she doing? She wasn't Juliet. She didn't know this guy. Neither did Ann for that matter.

Or had they talked on the phone already?

Would he know Kelly's voice wasn't Ann's? The one line greeting on the answering machine wouldn't be enough to give her away…would it?

She closed her eyes and silently cursed herself.

"You're there," he murmured, the words soft but at the same time somehow dangerous…or maybe she was imagining that part. Sexy. He sounded sexy…not dangerous.

"I…I was…yes," she stammered, the blood roaring so loud in her ears that she couldn't even hear herself think. She couldn't afford to start seeing bad guys around every corner.

"I'm glad you're home." There was a smile in his voice. "I was beginning to think you'd forgotten…or maybe that you'd changed your mind about tonight."

For a stranger he sounded awfully sincere…but could she trust her instincts right now? Maybe she wasn't thinking clearly. She shouldn't have picked up the phone…but there was always the chance he knew things about Ann that she didn't. Was it easier to open up to a name in a chat box…to a faceless entity that represented whatever your imagination conjured? He might be able to provide some insight to the inconsistencies Kelly had discovered. But she doubted that.

Yet she had to take the chance.

He was her only connection to Ann.

"No," she said, forcing strength into her voice. "I didn't change my mind. I…when are you coming over?" She had to assume that he knew Ann's address as well as her telephone number. Then again…what if they were supposed to meet some place? She had no idea. He would know she wasn't Ann. She prayed whoever was at the door couldn't hear her talking on the phone.

"I'm here now," the caller said on a chuckle. "That's me knocking at your door." He rapped his knuckles against the wood for emphasis. "I was beginning to think that maybe you didn't want to meet me."

Kelly placed the receiver back in its cradle without responding. Grappling for her scattered composure, she took a deep breath and walked to the door. She didn't even want to consider what he thought about her right now. She reached for the doorknob and shook her head in self-reproach. Whatever conclusions he'd formed about Ann, Kelly doubted she had lived up to a single one of them so far.

Pushing a smile into place, she opened the door. Felix scampered in, his tail twitching as he glided past her. The instant her gaze locked with Romeo's the idea that perhaps he and Ann had exchanged pictures over the Internet broadsided her.

Damn.

For five full seconds he stared at her without speaking or moving. In that seemingly endless lapse of time her anxiety level skyrocketed. Would he call the police? Would he demand to know what she'd done with Ann? Her heart stuttered to a complete stop at the next possibility. Would they think she had killed her friend?

She hadn't thought of that.

Did running from the scene make her look guilty of the crime that had taken place? She felt her eyes go wide. Of course it did. Dear God, how would she prove her innocence?

The television dramas and big screen films depicting crime scene investigations reeled through her mind like an out-of-control home movie. Gunpowder residue. Was it too late for them to test her hands for it? Prints? The guy had worn gloves, leaving no prints. The weapon? They would simply assume that she'd disposed of the weapon.

They would never believe her story.

But what about motive?

Why would she have killed her boss and friend?

Because she was jealous of her friend, wanted her life…? With morbid certainty she knew that's what they would say. And, to some degree, they would be right. She had envied Ann's life…envied her self-confidence and effortless beauty. But she would never have killed her for any reason. Another thought struck her. They would even use the lack of documentation about the real Ann Jones against her, assuming she had destroyed evidence.

She was doomed.

"Why didn't you warn me?"

The question jerked her from the disturbing ruminations. "Excuse me?" Had he figured her out already? Maybe he hadn't been fooled for a second. Maybe that's why he'd been staring at her without uttering another word. She'd stayed here too long…she should have figured out some other place to go before now. The police surely knew by now that the female murder victim they had in the morgue wasn't her. Now she was caught…caught before she could discover the identity of the evil that had taken her friend's life as well as her boss's.

"You were less than truthful when you said you were attractive," the Romeo staring at her so intently said in that deep, husky baritone that sent goose bumps over her skin.

Her breath trapped in her throat. He knew. He'd been expecting Ann's sophisticated elegance. Kelly possessed none. "I'm…" She shrugged and averted her gaze. "I don't know…" She summoned her courage and looked back into those assessing blue eyes "…what to say to that."

"You're downright gorgeous. That would have been clear enough." A grin eased across his lips, making those blue eyes sparkle magically. "For you." He offered her the fragrant bouquet of flowers he held.

For heaven's sake, she hadn't noticed the flowers. She'd been too busy staring at his face. Even now she found the task of shifting her gaze from that mesmerizing mosaic of perfection difficult. Chiseled jaw, full lips, a perfectly straight nose balanced squarely between the bluest eyes she'd ever seen. Throw in the thick brown hair and incredibly broad shoulders and anything else was pretty much insignificant.

She blinked, startled by her inability to think clearly. "Thank you." She accepted the flowers and tried to remember if she'd seen a vase anywhere in the house. Ann would know where she kept her vases. If she planned to carry on with this ruse—

A blast of cool air snapped her from her mental rambling. "I'm sorry." She stepped back. "Would you like to come in?" Already it was glaringly apparent that she was no good at this kind of subterfuge.

His smile was utterly charming and contagious. She found herself smiling back as he closed the door behind him. "Nice place," he commented.

She glanced around the entry hall and confessed that it was, indeed, a nice place. Ann's taste didn't disappoint. Not even her taste in men, Kelly mused, as she surveyed this Romeo from head to toe. Very tall, six-three or four maybe. Nice build, broad shoulders, narrow waist and muscular thighs that filled out the well-fitting jeans he wore. A crisp white shirt and aged leather jacket gave him a polished look. But it was the well-worn boots that made her heart skip a beat. All that was missing was the cowboy hat.

"I always leave my hat in the truck when paying a visit on a lady," he told her, as if reading her mind. But then, she hadn't made it difficult. She'd been staring at him practically from the moment she'd opened the door.

She nodded mutely and dragged her attention down to the flowers in her arms. Pulling it together about now would be a good thing. How could she expect to learn anything useful if she kept behaving like an idiot?

"Since we agreed to meet," he said, drawing her gaze back to his, "and I do have your address and telephone number, don't you think it's time we revealed our true identities?"

She blinked, startled by the wording of his request. "Of...course. Ann Jones." The lie rolled off her tongue a good deal more smoothly than she'd expected. She offered her hand. "And you are?"

"Trent Tucker." He took her hand in his but instead of shaking it he brushed his lips across her knuckles. She shivered. "A pleasure to meet you, Ann Jones." A breath-stealing grin spread mischievously across that handsome face yet again. He was enjoying her discomfort.

Kelly tugged her hand from his gentle but firm grip. "I'll get these in water." She gestured to the living room. "Make yourself comfortable. I'll only be a minute."

She executed an about-face and all but ran into the kitchen without a single backward glance. He could find his way to the sofa without any assistance from her and she needed a moment to gather her wits more firmly about her. She drew up short in the middle of the gourmet kitchen. There were dozens of cabinets. All she needed was a vase or, hell, a Texas-size glass, for these flowers.

Abandoning the bundle on the counter she decided to check beneath the sink first. If she had a vase in her town house that's where she'd keep it. No luck.

She checked door after door, finally discovering a lovely cut crystal vase behind the final door next to the walk-in pantry. Kelly breathed a sigh of relief as she filled the vase. Ann never cooked. What did she need with a kitchen like this? Granite counters, natural stone floors and tumbled marble backsplashes. Dozens upon dozens of cupboards and stainless steel commercial grade appliances.

Maybe she liked the image of "having it all" the ritzy condo gave her. Or maybe she just liked the location and didn't care what kind of kitchen it included. There didn't have to be a logical explanation for the woman's choice of decor. The condo likely came equipped this way.

She had to stop obsessing over insignificant details.

When she'd arranged the flowers as best she could, Kelly took a deep, resolute breath and prepared to face the stranger once more.

Why on earth had she answered that phone? He would have gone away, assuming that something had come up or that Ann had changed her mind. Why had she put herself in this position?

She hesitated in the entry hall and closed her eyes for one last moment of bravado building before she dived headlong into probable disaster. Because she was desperate. Desperate to reach out to someone…anyone who wasn't wearing a badge and knew anything at all about Ann.

Kelly couldn't be sure if Ann was the key to the mystery, but she had to start some place. Right now Romeo—Trent Tucker—was all she had.

TRENT SURVEYED the living room, taking in the details, pausing in his assessment to study the two framed photos on a table. Duplicates of the ones he'd seen at Kelly's apartment. Kelly Pruitt and Ann Jones at the beach and aboard the *Princess Ann*. The only things he'd noted thus far about Kelly Pruitt was that she looked even younger than her photos and she was as nervous as an armadillo trapped on I-10 in morning rush-hour traffic.

It hadn't taken Heath Murphy long to track down the two numbers called most frequently from Kelly Pruitt's apartment. Ray Jarvis's office and the Galveston house of one Ann Jones. A quick check with the DMV and Heath had learned that Ann Jones and Annie Sutton were either one in the same or identical twins. But, oddly, Heath hadn't been able to dig up anything else on the Jones alias. No date of birth or social security number. Just the driver's license.

Considering the way Ann Jones had lived, she had either found herself a very lucrative position with the drug cartel or she had found some other scam to work. When Trent had spoken with Senator Lester, just before driving here, he'd learned that the Bureau had finally admitted that Jarvis's firm had connections to the cartel. The senator felt certain there was more but that's all the feds would share at this point. They feared it would adversely affect their ongoing case.

Trent didn't believe in coincidences. Ann Jones aka Annie Sutton, hadn't been in Jarvis's office by chance. He'd be willing to bet that she hadn't even befriended Kelly Pruitt spontaneously. The whole situation smelled like a setup to him. The only question was, where did Kelly fit into this puzzle? Was she completely innocent of wrongdoing? Or had she been recruited into the dirty business by her boss or friend?

Whatever the case, right now, she was running scared. Trent had to find a way to get close enough to prod the truth from her while keeping her safe from the hit man who would no doubt want to finish the job he'd started. Right now, Kelly Pruitt was the only connection he had to what happened that evening. The senator would keep the brass off Trent's back for a few days while he attempted to put the pieces together. But that's all Lester could promise. If H.P.D. or the feds got wind of Kelly's location, they would want her in custody. That would accomplish nothing—except to get her killed if her survival somehow got leaked to the press.

Whatever piece of the puzzle she unknowingly held, Trent needed it to solve this case. Lester wanted his friend's murderer brought to justice. He wanted this case resolved and any possible links to the cartel uncovered for further investigation.

Kelly Pruitt was the only starting place Trent had.

She entered the room, the flowers he'd given her sprouting from a long, slim vase. The corners of her mouth turned upward into a smile, but not before he saw that luscious bottom lip quiver with the effort.

"It was sweet of you to bring flowers," she said, her voice as strained as the cheerful expression on her face. She set the arrangement on the coffee table in front of the sofa and clasped her hands nervously. Again he noted a tremor, this time in her hands before she restrained them.

Trent felt fairly certain she'd been holed up in this condo since fleeing the crime scene. He couldn't be sure if she'd kept up with the news reports regarding the murders, but either way she was growing desperate. That was the only explanation for her answering the phone when he called. Somehow she thought he could help her. Maybe she thought Romeo and Juliet—Ann—were closer than they actually were. Or maybe she simply needed human contact. She'd been completely alone since the murders if his conclusions were correct. If she was half as innocent as her past conveyed, she had to be scared to death.

"You said you liked a man who came bearing gifts," he reminded, uncertain as to whether Ann would have shared that information with her friend. The e-mails Heath had retrieved from her inbox indicated she'd said it to her online suitor. "Flowers might not have been what you had in mind, but it's a start."

She nodded jerkily. "Flowers are perfect."

He took two steps in her direction and she almost bolted. Damn, she was getting more antsy by the moment. He splayed his hand in question. "Maybe this setting is a little too intimate," he suggested knowingly. "Why don't we go out to dinner? We don't have to eat here."

Her eyes rounded with uncertainty. "I...I...we don't have to go out," she countered quickly.

Her pulse fluttered wildly at the base of her throat. He needed her out of here, in neutral territory. "I'd feel better about it if I took you to dinner rather than have you slave over a hot stove." He gave her his most reassuring smile. "I'd much prefer to enjoy your company without adding to the hassle."

She nodded stiffly. "Okay. Just…" She gestured to the stairs. "Just let me change."

Before he could argue that she looked fine just as she was, Kelly was halfway up the stairs. The urge to follow her and make sure she didn't make a run for it was nearly overwhelming. He'd blocked the garage to the condo with his rented four-wheel-drive truck. She wouldn't be leaving in the car she'd taken from the crime scene. But that didn't keep her from fleeing on foot.

Trent turned his attention back to the room and any details about the owner it might give away. He'd just have to take a chance on Kelly.

Even if she ran, he'd find her again.

KELLY LEANED against the closed bedroom door. She tried to slow her whirling thoughts and her pounding heart. She had to stay cool. Losing control would not help her situation. It was only dinner…at some local restaurant most likely. No one around here knew her. Though she had visited Ann a few times, certainly it hadn't been enough for her to be recognized by any of the locals.

She had nothing to worry about.

Except him.

She closed her eyes and released a heavy breath. He made her uneasy…restless. Nothing he'd said or done lent any credibility to her reaction. It was simply his intense presence. Admittedly, he was everything she'd dreamed of some day finding in a man. Handsome, kind, strong, soft-spoken. But he wasn't here for her. He was here for Ann. Not to mention the second the police figured out she was still alive, she would be a murder suspect.

She shuddered then pushed away from the door and went to the closet. How had this happened? What was Ray or Ann or both into that could cause this kind of chain reaction? She shuddered again when the sound of those hissing pops echoed in her head. Had Ray recognized his killer as he took his last breath? Had he known it could happen? Maybe that's why he'd been so nervous that evening. Kelly had never seen him so agitated. He had been scared. Whether for the mistake he'd made or for some purposeful wrongdoing, she couldn't be sure. She'd never known him to behave that way.

Forcing her attention back to the here and now, Kelly focused on the clothes lining the walk-in closet. What would Ann wear for her first date with the Romeo she'd courted for weeks now?

Kelly tried to remember all that her friend had said about her online beau. He liked things sexy. That's what she'd said. Kelly shivered. Sexy fit. The guy downstairs was definitely the kind of man who made a woman want to look sexy.

What was she thinking?

Kelly held the silky blouse she'd selected against her chest and shook her head. This guy could be a serial killer for all she knew. Why in God's name had she allowed him into the house? Just because Ann was foolish enough to make a date with him didn't mean she had to see it through.

But her friend was smarter than that. Wasn't she? She'd seemed so...so sophisticated and elegant, so smart. Surely she wouldn't be fooled easily.

Did that mean that all victims of killers were stupid or naive? Absolutely not or Ray and Ann wouldn't be lying in a morgue on a cold slab at this very moment. Kelly winced at the mental pictures that thought evoked. Damn she'd made a mistake.

Kelly grabbed a pair of emerald green slacks to match the blouse and quickly dressed. She might as well get this over with. He was here. She couldn't change that glaring fact. The truth was she'd overstayed her welcome anyway. She shouldn't have come here. Eventually the police would show up. She couldn't be so naive as to believe that she could merely pretend to be Ann permanently. She had to find out what really happened.

Nothing in Ann's apartment, other than the surprising discovery that she could access some of Ray's files from her home computer, could be of any use to Kelly. Tonight, after she'd gotten rid of Romeo, she'd pack a few things, including Ann's laptop and cell phone and she'd get out of town.

When she felt far enough away, she'd hide the car and purchase a bus ticket to...anywhere.

She stared at her reflection as she tugged a brush through her shoulder-length hair. And what would that accomplish? She'd still be a fugitive and her friends would still be dead. And where would she get the money?

There was only one way to clear up this mess. She had to find out who Ray and/or Ann had gotten involved with. Someone evil enough to order their murders, not to mention the murder of an assistant who knew nothing of the presumed wrongdoing.

The other man who'd died in Ray's office was FBI. Could she trust the FBI if she went to them? The news had reported that the agent's office was in Dallas. She could go to Dallas…check out the situation.

But if the FBI could be trusted—if they had the capability of protecting their own—why was Agent Davis dead?

Her movements on autopilot, she picked through Ann's makeup drawer until she found some blush and lip gloss. Just a little something to provide some color to her pale complexion. She stared into her weary, solemn eyes as she applied the cosmetics. What was she going to do?

The police and the FBI couldn't help her because they didn't know anymore than she did. Otherwise one or both would be touting to the media the names of suspects or the steps being taken to solve the case. And one of their own wouldn't be dead.

Nope. They didn't have squat.

What Kelly really needed was a private detective.

For that she had to have money.

Her savings would be enough.

But could a dead woman make a withdrawal at her financial institution?

Chapter Six

Trent was relatively certain he'd never seen anyone suffer so immensely and yet so graciously through a meal. Kelly, still calling herself Ann, had even managed to eat a bite or two, but mostly she kept looking around the restaurant as if she feared being recognized.

Which was exactly the problem, he knew without question.

She picked at her decadent chocolate dessert while he consumed his with almost as much insatiableness as his gaze devoured the sight of her. Damn, he hated admitting that weakness, but it was true. He'd felt a blow to his equilibrium the instant he'd laid eyes on her. The photographs definitely hadn't done her justice. But that little off-kilter sensation had been nothing compared with the sense of gut-wrenching lust he'd experienced when she'd appeared on the second-story landing after changing for dinner. He'd had trouble keeping his eyes as well as his thoughts on anything else since she'd descended the stairs wearing that shimmery emerald outfit.

The color brought out the most incredible flecks of green in her hazel eyes. The silky texture of the fabric only served to enhance the creaminess of her skin. The blond tresses of pure temptation drifting over her shoulders made him itch to run his fingers through it. As if all those things weren't bad enough, that mouth of hers made him want to drag her across the table here and now and plaster his lips possessively over it.

He was thirty-three and not once in his life had he been this caught off guard by a woman before. Well, okay, he'd been physically attracted on sight to his share but not on this level. This was…intense. The chemistry between them was clearly magnified by the situation. He almost patted himself on the back for coming up with that one. Made sense though. She was a woman in jeopardy—or trouble, depending upon what his investigation revealed—and she had this whole demeanor of innocence about her. This ethereal cloak of sweetness.

Maybe he'd been living in the north too long. He'd apparently forgotten how naive and innocent a young Texas belle could be if she so chose. According to her background info, she'd grown up in a small east Texas town, only coming to Houston after she'd graduated college. Looking for bigger and better things, he presumed.

Whatever charms she possessed, natural or honed over time, she was playing havoc with his ability to concentrate.

The air was different down here, he reminded himself in consolation. He just didn't have his cowboy legs back under him yet. He'd grown up in Texas, had made a good living tracking fugitives all across this great state. But he'd given that life up three years ago when he'd moved north. Texas wasn't home anymore...it was just the place where his latest assignment had taken him.

He had to remember that.

He forced the gloom of the past from his thoughts and focused on the lady currently navigating her fork around the edges of a slice of triple layer chocolate cake, slathered with fudge icing and drizzled with raspberry sauce.

"Are you going to eat that or play with it?" he asked, one eyebrow cocked in a challenge. Didn't all girls south of the Mason-Dixon line know it was a mortal sin to waste a treat like that?

A smile peeked from behind her grim expression. "I'm sorry. Do you want it?" She shoved the white bone china plate in his direction. "I'm stuffed."

Now she sounded like a northern girl. "You've barely touched it," he chastised as he dipped his finger in the raspberry sauce and licked it appreciatively.

She followed the movement with avid curiosity. "I...well." She cleared her throat daintily. "I guess I'm just not that hungry."

Murder had a way of doing that to a person, he mused, then chastised himself for being less than charitable. But it was his only protection against...her lure.

"Why don't you tell me what brought you to Houston?" he ventured before shoveling a healthy portion of her dessert into his mouth.

She picked up her cup, held it in both hands and sipped the lukewarm coffee in an attempt to evade his question.

"Didn't you say you'd moved here a couple of years ago?" he prodded, then gulped a swallow of his own coffee.

She nodded. "From Dallas," she answered without meeting his eyes. "I grew up in Dallas."

Lying wasn't pleasurable to her. He was glad to see that. Anyone who could lie straight-faced and not flinch couldn't be trusted on any level. This was the second time today he'd seen her struggle with an untruth.

"What about you?" She did look at him then, a spark of defiance in her eyes. Feeling helpless was another thing she didn't much care for. "What is it you do, Trent?"

So this vulnerable little girl who had delusions of finding the quintessential cowboy had a little fight in her after all. Not that he'd actually doubted it. It took guts to run from a murder scene and hide out for days. Most would consider it a cowardly act, but he knew better. She might be running but she wasn't a coward. Kelly Pruitt had a plan. Every instinct told him that she knew something—suspected something—and intended to pursue it. That's what tonight was all about. She was reaching out to the only connection she had to her dead friend.

If he had her pegged right, she was looking for the same thing he was. But he couldn't be positive just yet. So, for now, he'd have to keep up the pretense.

"I'm an investigative journalist," he responded,

setting his cover into place. "But I'm taking a few months off to work on my first novel."

"You're a writer? How interesting. What kind of writing do you do?"

She relaxed marginally. Good. "I cover the police beat for the *Chicago Tribune,* homicide investigation mostly."

Her posture stiffened slightly. "Really. I imagine that can get pretty gruesome."

"That's the downside," he agreed. "Still, my work has helped me forge some beneficial relationships within the field and since I plan to pen a murder mystery, I guess it's a good thing."

Anticipation lit up those pretty eyes. "So you know your way around a murder investigation."

"Too well," he admitted. He'd seen far too many ugly scenes like the one she'd lived through. One in particular had changed his life permanently. He never wanted to get that close to death again. Not when the situation was out of his control. If he was going to get involved with that kind of case, like now with Kelly Pruitt, he would be in charge. Every step would be his decision.

Without warning she scooted her seat back and stood. "Excuse me."

She was hurrying across the dining room before he could fully react. Dropping back into his own chair, he watched her disappear into the corridor marked Rest Rooms. The subject of murder had sent her running. Was she getting closer to the edge? Ready to admit what she'd seen, what she knew?

The possibility that she might run from what she

perceived as a threat—his knowledge of murder investigations—had him leaving some cash on the table and following the direction she'd taken.

KELLY HEAVED again and again but there was nothing left to expel from her churning stomach. She eased down onto the floor and sagged against the stall.

After three days the reality had suddenly hit her…right in the middle of dessert with a stranger.

As he'd talked about his profession, image after image had abruptly flashed in her mind. Ann. Her white blouse soaked in bright red blood. Ray with that hole in him, blood leaking down his shirtfront. And then that other man. She shuddered and her stomach spasmed again. A good portion of the back of his head had been missing.

The killer had intended to kill her as well…thought he had. She was as good as dead if he got wind that she'd survived. But even more devastating, there didn't appear to be anything she could do to help her friends.

She'd found nothing at Ann's apartment other than the access to Ray's files. She couldn't decipher the disk. And this man clearly knew no more about Ann than she did. Not as much actually.

What was she going to do?

She couldn't trust anyone.

Not once in her life had she felt this totally helpless. Even when she'd lost her parents, so close together, she'd known she could work through it. Had formed a plan and focused on what needed to be done.

But this was different.

There was nothing she could do to make this right...to fix this.

She hoisted herself up and dusted off her clothes. Sitting here feeling sorry for herself wasn't going to help. She had to do something. Get back to Ann's and work on the disk. Who knows? She could get lucky and figure out the password. Maybe she could go on the Internet and look for some code busters. They sold everything else on there.

After washing her hands she finger-combed her hair and pinched her cheeks to add a little pink to her otherwise ghastly pale face. She rinsed her mouth again but the water just wasn't working on the rancid taste left behind. With no other option she sudsed her finger with hand soap and scrubbed her teeth and tongue with that. After several more rinses she could tolerate the lingering hint of soap that managed to overpower the other.

Kelly took a couple of deep breaths and rolled her neck. Okay. She could do this. All she had to do was keep it together until Trent took her back to Ann's place.

She marched to the door, telling herself over and over again that she was strong...she was tougher than this. Throwing open the door she stepped into the corridor, her composure back in place now.

He was there, waiting for her. Her purse dangling from one very masculine hand.

"You okay?"

The tears came on suddenly but she blinked them back, determined not to humiliate herself further.

"I'm fine." She went for a smile but it stretched flatly across her face, falling well short of the mark.

"I'll take you home now," he offered.

She nodded, not sure if her voice would hold steady for her to say anything in response to that.

The truth was she couldn't go home. Who knew if she even had a home anymore? The world thought she was dead. The landlady had likely already started packing up her goods for claiming by next of kin. Kelly doubted that either of her cousins would bother with coming all the way to Texas to claim her belongings, much less her body.

The cold hard reality of that thought hit her head-on. Today was Monday. A holiday. By tomorrow or the next for sure, someone would come. The police would insist on someone identifying her body. How else would they do it? She knew the usual ways depicted on the television crime dramas. Dental records and fingerprints. She had no prints on file anywhere. But she had been to the dentist regularly for most of her adult life. She didn't know how the police located a person's dentist, maybe from receipts in their home, or whatever, but hers was right here in Houston.

The bottom line was she was out of time.

Tomorrow her dentist would be back in his office. If they didn't already know she wasn't dead, they would by this time tomorrow.

As they exited the lobby area Kelly snagged a peppermint from the table next to the maître d'. She popped it into her mouth and tried to focus on the sweet taste. Her gaze shifted to the tall man holding the door open for her. This night was almost over.

She might as well enjoy the perk of admiring such a fine specimen of the male species a few minutes longer. Texas prisons weren't known for their attractive guards, and she'd never met a mortician period, let alone one she found attractive. And, considering she was likely either going to prison or to hell, she should savor this moment.

He commented on how nice the moon looked reflecting on the water as they drove along Lakeside. She made a sound of agreement but she wasn't really listening. Instead, she studied the way the lights from the dash and the moon, and even the occasional streetlamp, enhanced the planes and angles of his face. She'd always considered that a guy as tall as him, as *big* as him, would be too much to still be attractive. But she'd been wrong. He didn't look overly tall or overly large in any way. He looked extremely well proportioned and he moved with a kind of ease and grace that defied explanation for a man of his size. Yet, the most unsettling quality, she decided, was his voice. Deep and gentle, again in utter contrast to his stature. She especially liked that about him.

She wondered what made a terrific-looking guy with, as far as she could tell, a great personality seek out companionship on the Internet. Like everything else in her life lately, it didn't make sense.

"Why the Internet?" The question slipped out before she could stop it.

He glanced at her, those blue eyes catching the meager light and somehow reflecting it. The smile took her breath. That she'd pretty much gotten used to. The man knew how to smile.

"I could ask you the same," he remarked, letting the challenge hang in the air.

Just when she'd decided he wasn't going to say more, he continued, "I let work get in the way. Always too busy for a typical social life. I used the Net so much in my research." He lifted a shoulder in a shrug. "It was just easy."

She nodded. Sounded reasonable. "Is this your first date with someone from…like me?"

That smile again. "Yeah. This is the first and only time."

Something about that confession touched her more deeply than anything else he'd said since they met. She suddenly wanted to ask him a dozen questions…to know more about him, but they were back at the condo. He climbed from behind the wheel and hustled around to her door.

"It's warmer tonight," he noted as he walked her to the door. "Nice."

Winter in south Texas was generally fairly mild. Certainly a drastic change from Chicago.

"Well, thanks for dinner." The smile that moved across her face this time was real, felt good after so many days of nothing to smile about. She'd enjoyed the time with him. Appreciated the distraction, up until the end.

His expression turned serious then. "I hope I'll see you again. I'll be in town for a while longer."

She hadn't thought of that. He'd be going back to Chicago eventually. She supposed he was here on research or visiting friends or relatives. Had he said so and she'd simply missed it?

"I'd like that," she admitted. Might as well, she couldn't possibly do anything any more humiliating than that dash for the bathroom. She certainly didn't have anything to lose. And it beat the heck out of sulking around this house.

"I'll call then."

She nodded. But would she be here? she considered abruptly. It wasn't safe for her to stay here any longer. She knew that. Why press her luck? That reality was something she couldn't share with him. However much she suddenly wanted to.

"Goodnight, Juliet," he murmured.

Startled at his use of that name, she looked up at him just as his mouth descended toward hers. Her heart shuddered to a near stop as those amazing lips brushed against hers. He kissed her softly, tenderly. His touch reminded her of the way he spoke, slow, gentle, and so sexy she could hardly stand the divine torture.

When he drew back she had to lean against the door to stay vertical. "Sleep well," he whispered before walking away.

She wanted to call out to him, to tell him goodnight or goodbye…anything. But she couldn't make her lips form the words. They were still burning up from his kiss.

The one he'd whispered on her lips.

TRENT WATCHED as Kelly moved about in the bedroom upstairs. He could see her silhouette against the window and every muscle in his body went rigid with flat-out lust. He'd thought he couldn't get any harder but he'd been wrong. For half an hour now he'd been watching the condo, concentrating on relaxing the way his body had reacted to hers. He didn't get it. It was just a kiss, barely one at that. And yet, he couldn't slow this raging hard-on. Every move she made tightened the noose of need around his neck.

He wanted her. It was that simple. He couldn't name the motivation. Sure she was gorgeous, but he'd worked around gorgeous women before. She was running for her life, well that was nothing new. He'd rescued plenty of damsels in distress in his time.

It had to be the sheer innocence she radiated. The vulnerability that made him want to protect her beyond a professional level.

He'd spent the past twenty-four hours analyzing her and her background, looking at pictures of her, forming scenarios to align with her actions. But nothing had prepared him for this kind of physical reaction. He knew better than to get personally involved with a client or a suspect, and she was the latter.

Trent sighed and relaxed more fully into the seat. He'd never been one to deny the truth. He had a serious problem here, but he felt reasonably sure he could handle it. Maybe by tomorrow the haze of lust would fade, lessen somewhat. He could hope.

He'd parked his truck in the driveway of a neighboring house directly across the street. The owners were out of town judging by the accumulated mail in their box. He supposed they could return sometime during the night and then he'd simply leave before they could ask any questions. Sleep wasn't on his agenda. He planned to keep an eye on Kelly Pruitt.

He had a gut feeling that she was on the verge of running again.

Wherever she went, he intended to be right behind her.

SPECIAL AGENT Cyrus McCade, better known as Mac to his buddies in the Bureau, got comfortable on his sofa and studied the report he'd received on one Trent Tucker of the Colby Agency in Chicago.

A native of Texas, Mr. Tucker had shut down his thriving bounty hunter business after a double homicide in El Paso that he apparently considered his fault. He'd tracked down a scumbag repeat felon only to have the courts let him go free again. Tucker had known the man's wife and daughter were in danger since the wife had given him the man's location previously, landing him in jail. But no one had listened to Tucker and while he was out on another retrieval, the bastard was cut loose, and his wife and daughter were dead before dark that same day.

He tossed the report aside and reached for his drink. Damn shame, Mac mused as he surfed the satellite channels for something worth watching on Monday night. But then the bitch shouldn't have sold her husband out. The kid, well that was a different story. Mac had no use for assholes that harmed children, but the wife—in his opinion she got what she deserved. Just like that whore Ann Jones, Annie Sutton, or whatever the hell she liked calling herself was going to get hers.

She'd almost screwed him royally. But he'd headed off her ploy. Now all he had to do was make the

others see it. Since the hit on Jarvis's office she had
been laying low in her place in Galveston, but she
would get hers. He'd see to it. Right now, however,
he had bigger problems.

What the hell was some hotshot P.I. from Chicago
doing nosing around in his territory? In an H.P.D.
investigation? He had a bad feeling that it had something to do with the senator. He'd been nosing
around, too.

Hell, Mac was barely keeping his head above water
with this damned internal affairs investigation.
Couldn't a guy with twenty years under his belt have
a few discrepancies in his case reports? What was the
big deal?

He smiled, giving himself a mental pat on the back.
He'd covered his ass well enough. Let Davis take the
fall. Six months from now they'd still be scratching
their heads trying to figure that one out. Jarvis was
dirty, they would conclude, though they would never
find hardcore evidence. Davis had been facilitating his
efforts in some way, taking kickbacks. Mac even had
a Dallas prostitute prepared to testify that the young,
seemingly clean agent, had been keeping her up for
more than a year now. Wouldn't that just finish off
his reputation?

The thing that mattered was that the job was done.
That whining jerk Jarvis was out of the way. The
accounts were covered. And no one had a damned
thing on Mac or the cartel. Ann's fate was yet to be
determined. Personally, he wanted to give her what
she'd been asking for now for months and then he
wanted to kill her. She'd negotiated long enough for

the cartel to know how to do her job. Her bumbling with Jarvis was pure negligence. If the cartel let her slide, he'd be tempted to handle it privately.

But that would likely get him offed in a similar manner.

He'd just have to live with whatever the powers that be decided. Sometimes the guys with the money and power had the least brains.

Wasn't nothing to him. As long as he got his cut like clockwork, he'd keep the feds off the cartel. He'd already set up a small organized crime family working out of Dallas to take the fall for this whole screw-up. That too could get him killed, but he wasn't worried. The cartel would take care of him as long as they needed him. And he had every intention of seeing that they needed him for a long time to come.

The only fly in the ointment was the damned P.I. Mac had to find out what he was up to. He'd already reached out and touched a few of his sources. Whatever word was out he'd hear soon enough.

As if fate had been listening his cell phone rang. He pressed the mute button on the television remote and shifted to a better position on the sofa. "Mc-Cade," he grunted when he'd flipped open his phone.

"You're not going to believe this."

Mac perked up. "Whatcha got, Kennamer?" Kennamer worked homicide for H.P.D. He'd earned his detective shield last year, though Mac couldn't see how. All he could think was that the precinct was hard up for reliable cops. At least the dirtbag was good for something.

"That P.I. you asked me about," Kennamer begun,

"he lit a fire under Hargrove and had him checking into the female victim in the Jarvis murder case."

Mac frowned. What the hell for? The bitch was dead. Besides, the assistant didn't know a damned thing. "What was the point in that little exercise?"

"Who knows?" Kennamer snorted, clearing his draining sinuses. "Anyway, Hargrove ran her prints and guess what?"

Mac rolled his eyes. "What?"

"She's not Kelly Pruitt, Jarvis's assistant."

Mac sat up straighter. "Who the hell is she then?" A dozen scenarios, all bad, reeled through his mind like a bad movie.

"Some broad named Annie Sutton, got busted for dope seven years ago."

Fear trickled through Mac. Annie Sutton, aka Ann Jones. Former dopehead turned power player. "What's Hargrove doing about this?" Hargrove was the best detective the homicide division had, not that the designation was saying much. Still, if there was anything to find he'd be the most likely one to find it.

"He won't say," Kennamer related. "He's keeping everything hush-hush now. Orders from Senator Lester."

Mac swore under his breath. "Thanks, Kennamer. I owe you one."

When he'd ended the call, Mac sat on the edge of his couch and considered the ramifications of this little turn of events. He shook his head. Couldn't anybody do anything right anymore?

The cartel had sent their best cleanup man to do the job. What the hell went wrong?

The way Mac saw it that was the cartel's problem.

He flipped open his phone to make the call. He'd driven to Galveston Saturday night, had watched the upstairs light go on and then off in the condo to make sure Ann was following orders to stay put. She'd been told not to interfere with the hit on Jarvis's office. He'd thought she had heeded those instructions.

He punched in the necessary numbers and waited out the rings. If Ann was dead that meant only one thing, the person occupying her condo was Kelly Pruitt.

Chapter Seven

Trent rolled out of the neighboring driveway just after daylight. There was a small diner a few blocks away and that was his destination. He went inside and placed an order for two breakfasts, including steaming coffee, then headed to the rest room.

Inside he took care of necessary business, then shaved using the cordless shaver he carried for times just like this, and brushed his teeth. With a shirt change, some fresh aftershave and deodorant, he was good to go. He ran his fingers through his hair for good measure and stuffed yesterday's shirt as well as his toiletries back into his duffel.

He picked up the order and drove back to the condo. This time he pulled into the driveway. He knocked three times and identified himself before she opened the door.

She looked bleary-eyed and no more rested than she had the night before. The fluffy white robe was pulled tight around her and he couldn't help wondering what she wore underneath. "Trent? Did we discuss breakfast?'' she asked, noting the bag and carrier containing coffee cups in his hands.

He smiled, giving it all the charm he could produce without having had a cup of coffee. ''I couldn't wait to see you again.''

Looking doubtful, she stepped back and allowed him inside. ''It smells great,'' she admitted grudgingly.

She led the way to the kitchen and he quickly spread the bounty on the counter. She was right about the smell, it made him realize just how hungry he was.

Unfortunately, he confessed to himself as she sat down across from him, food wasn't the only thing on his mind. He'd hoped that he would see things differently this morning, that he wouldn't feel that same intensity when in her presence, but he did. The moment she'd opened the door and peered up at him, heat had seared through him, making his skin feel too tight and his lower anatomy too tense. Focusing on the food, he ordered his body to relax. Going down that road would be a mistake, one he'd never made and never intended to.

Kelly's appetite was back this morning. It was the first time she'd felt hungry since…since Friday. She supposed it was survival instinct kicking in. She had to eat to survive.

She hadn't slept well last night. All the details that didn't make sense kept playing over and over in her mind. But it just wouldn't gel. The idea that she needed help, professional help in the way of a P.I., had niggled her once or twice. But then, the news this morning had really driven the point home. The authorities were intensifying their investigation. Certain new, undisclosed evidence had been discovered. She had a bad feeling that *she* was that new evidence. She had to do something!

Trent wasn't a private investigator, but he was an investigative reporter. He'd told her that he'd worked closely with the detectives on numerous homicide cases. He knew the routine, had connections. He could help her. She was certain of it. She had to give it a shot. Desperation was tightening its hold on her.

"Did you hear or read about those Houston murders at that investment firm last Friday?" she asked. She watched his reaction closely, gauging to see if she should say more.

He shrugged then reached for his coffee. "I may have seen something about it in the paper." He took a hefty swallow before settling that analyzing gaze on her. "What happened?"

Now he was the one gauging, assessing. She moistened her lips and told herself that she didn't really have any choice. She had to do something. She was out of options and time. She'd had no luck with the disk, couldn't trust the police. "I...I knew them."

"That's just awful." His hand covered hers and he squeezed comfortingly. "How is the investigation going? Have you heard if they have any suspects?"

Her gaze met his as anticipation and anxiety reached an all-time high inside her. "I was there."

The statement hung in the air for a long moment.

"You were there—in the office—when the murders occurred?" he asked gently.

She blinked back the tears that threatened. She did so appreciate that gentleness right now. Only then did it occur to her that the reason was because her father had always spoken gently that way. She almost smiled, her emotions teetering on some unfamiliar precipice. This man reminded her of her father. That's why she felt so close to him. Why had she only just now realized that? Too much happening...she couldn't cope with all of it.

"I was there," she confirmed. Not quite ready to tell him the whole truth, she left her identity concealed. "Mr. Jarvis was in his office in a meeting with another man and I was at the reception desk with my friend." She thought back to those final moments before...before those lethal sounds of death had hissed through the air.

"She had to use the phone and I dropped... something on the floor." The pictures played out in her mind in slow motion. Her reaching to retrieve the disk, Ann inadvertently knocking it farther under the desk. "I crouched down to pick it up but I couldn't reach it, so I had to kind of crawl under the desk." The tinkle of the bell. "I heard someone come into the lobby. The bell over the door jingled." Two consecutive hissing pops. "Before I could get up she fell." Her gaze connected with Trent's. "I cowered under the desk while she lay there bleeding to death." She gestured to her chest. "It happened so fast. Her eyes...were open. She didn't move."

The door to her boss's office opened in her mind, the sound drawing her back to that moment. "I heard him go into Mr. Jarvis's office. I wanted to scream…to warn him but it was too late." More deadly sounds. "And then it was over."

"Did you see the man who fired the shots?" Trent asked quietly.

She shook her head. "I couldn't see anything." She shuddered at the memory of him coming over to her desk, hanging up the phone. "He had on black pants and boots. You know…" she grappled for the right word "…the combat kind. And he wore gloves. I saw his hand when he hung up the phone she'd been using."

"Tell me what happened next."

Slowly, with a few false starts and overwhelming moments, she told him the rest. About the killer's phone call and then about hiding in the vent duct while the office was searched.

"So you've been in hiding ever since," he guessed.

She nodded. "I can't see how anything I could tell the police would help the case. I didn't see any of their faces. I didn't recognize the voices and I have no idea what they were looking for."

She'd opted not to mention the disk for the time being. She had to take this one step at a time. Telling him what she had so far had taken a great deal of courage. He was a stranger…but one she somehow trusted.

Maybe because Ann had trusted him enough to give him her address and telephone number. Maybe simply because she was attracted to him. She thought about that kiss and how it had affected her. But she had to remember one very important thing, that kiss had been for Ann. He thought she was Ann. None of his attention was for her. But, if he could help her, she would play the part as long as necessary.

TRENT ANALYZED all that she'd said to him while the remainder of their breakfast got cold. But his appetite had been overridden by his investigator's instincts humming to life. No wonder Kelly had run for her life. She knew as well as he did that no professional hit man would allow a loose end once he discovered it. The moment her survival was made public her life wouldn't be worth two cents.

He had to touch base with Hargrove and make absolutely certain the man kept a lid on the female victim's identity. The senator could help with that.

"You don't know of any reason someone would want to murder Mr. Jarvis and his assistant?" he asked, wording his question carefully so as not to alarm her or arouse her suspicion.

She shook her head, then frowned. "I can only imagine that it would have something to do with an illegal transfer of money." She shrugged. "Money laundering for bad guys maybe?"

Did she know more than she was telling? He had a feeling she did. "Did you have reason to suspect Mr. Jarvis of this type of activity?"

She shook her head. "No way. He was a good guy. I think if he was involved it was a mistake…an accident. I think maybe that's why there was an FBI agent there. Ray—Mr. Jarvis probably called him in for his advice on the situation or to start an investigation."

She obviously didn't know about the money in the

agent's pocket. "That's possible." In Trent's opinion it was not only possible but also probable. The money in the envelope was just too convenient.

"And your friend," Trent inquired cautiously, "is there any chance she was involved?"

Kelly thought about that for a while before answering. He suspected she was searching for a way to phrase her response.

"I think it's possible." She looked at him briefly, careful not to maintain eye contact as she spoke. "I found some files that I don't understand. A corporation called Renaissance. There was something about the way it was set up that gave me pause. I believe that was the client Mr. Jarvis suspected and, if so, it's definitely connected to my friend."

Trent committed the name of the corporation to memory so he could have Heath look into it. "I'll tell you what, why don't you get dressed and I'll make a few phone calls. Tap some of my sources and see what they recommend."

He was banking on her taking a shower. He needed some time to look around. The files she mentioned were likely here if they were connected to Ann. Accessing them was essential.

The tremulous smile that spanned those lush lips tied a dozen knots in his gut. "I'd appreciate that." She stood. "I'd like to take a shower if you don't mind."

"Take your time."

She started to clean up the mess but he stopped her. "I'll get it."

Her smile wavering just a little beneath the weight

of some other emotion he couldn't quite define, she nodded and left him to the chore.

Trent made quick work of disposing of the remnants of their meal. Taking a moment to ensure she had closed the door to her room, he started his search. He didn't bother with the kitchen and the cursory perusal he gave the living room revealed nothing. The office was where he wanted to focus. He scanned the desk drawers and file cabinets, finding nothing that merited a second look. When he'd searched the office as thoroughly as he felt necessary, he listened again for sounds from the upstairs bedroom. The shower was running. Perfect.

He sat down at the desk and turned on the laptop stationed there. An error message stopped the start-up process and he discovered a disk in the drive. It was unmarked but could contain what he was looking for. As soon as the operating system was online, he viewed the contents of the disk. Several files were stored there but protected by a password. He didn't have time to attempt breaching the password. Instead he forwarded the files to Heath's inbox at the Colby Agency with a message requesting that he attempt to access the files. He also gave him the name of the corporation Kelly suspected.

Trent listened to see that she was still upstairs and then he surveyed the rest of the files on the laptop. When he'd forwarded to Heath anything that piqued his interest, he shut the system down and left it as he'd found it.

As he stood, Kelly appeared in the doorway.

He tensed inwardly, careful not to let her see his

reaction. "That was fast," he remarked casually as he allowed his approving gaze to rove over her in an effort to distract her from what she was no doubt thinking.

"Was there something you needed?" She looked from him to the desk, clearly suspicious.

"Just the telephone directory. I couldn't find one in the living room. It was in here. So I used the phone. I hope that was okay."

She surveyed the desk and then the nearby credenza verifying that the directory was, in fact, close by. "Sure. It's fine," she said then. "Look, if you don't mind taking me, there's someplace I'd like to go."

He stood and smiled down at her, enjoying the little shiver that went through her when she stared at his lips. "I'm yours for the day." Her gaze bumped into his once more. "Or for however long it takes."

She didn't have to say anything…he could read the appreciation, the relief, in her eyes. Kelly Pruitt needed a friend right now. Badly. And whether she fully realized it or not, she needed protection—even worse.

Portofino Harbor, she'd told him. Trent reasoned that a trip to a nearby harbor could only be connected with the *Princess Ann*. If there was any chance Ann had stashed something there he was all for the outing. It would definitely be worth the risk.

Allowing the tension to eddy from his shoulders, he stepped out onto the porch, first taking a quick look around before she emerged from the house. He didn't think anyone was watching them just yet, but he didn't like taking chances.

KELLY COULDN'T get past the feeling that Trent had been snooping in Ann's office. Though his explanation for being there was perfectly plausible, still…it didn't feel right. She glanced at him now as he drove away from the condo. That hard-jawed profile and those sturdy shoulders made her feel somehow safe and secure no matter what she'd thought moments ago. The very thought of being held in those strong arms made her quiver inside.

She forced her gaze to the passing landscape. Maybe the events of the past few days had pushed her over that edge she feared. Maybe this was all just a bad dream that she'd wake up from any minute now.

No such luck. It was real. She glanced at Trent. The good and the bad.

How could she be certain which one he was?

There were no certainties in any of this, she reasoned. But she had to trust someone. She couldn't do this alone.

Pointing her attention back to the here and now, she couldn't imagine that Ann had hidden anything aboard the *Princess Ann,* but it was the only place left to look. She hadn't really thought about that until this morning. She pretty much knew what was back at the office, and she'd searched Ann's condo from top to bottom. That left only the boat that she knew of.

She felt the desperation rise into her throat again

and she tamped it down. She had to focus. Had to find a way to look around without appearing suspicious since the boat was supposed to be hers. She just prayed he wouldn't ask which end was which because she'd never gotten starboard and port straight despite Ann's lessons.

When they reached the harbor, Trent parked and quickly came around to open her door. She liked that and took a moment to revel in the sweetness. The morning breeze was crisp, but it wasn't so bad. The temperature hovered around fifty degrees. She couldn't complain about that. She hugged her jacket close as they walked along the pier. Try as she might to focus on the matter at hand, she couldn't help staring at the man beside her. She wondered again why he rarely wore his hat. He had the cowboy way about him…but it wasn't quite complete.

He caught her looking at him and grinned. "You're going to have to stop doing that or I'm going to get ideas," he teased.

She grinned right back, hoping to camouflage her prodding remark within the light conversation. "I'm beginning to think that you only have that hat for show."

He paused, looked her straight in the eye, which rattled her to the point of losing her breath and stalled her feet as if the pier had turned to mire. "I'm a different kind of cowboy," he said softly. "Contrary to popular thinking, clothes don't make the man."

He had her there. Heat seared her cheeks, as much from his sensual tone as from embarrassment. An entirely different kind of heat warmed her insides.

"Touché," she mused before forcing her feet back into forward motion. She was here for a purpose and it didn't involve letting this tension-filled moment get out of hand. Her gaze zeroed in immediately on the slip where Ann's boat was moored.

"This way," she said to her companion.

The *Princess Ann* was a thirty-six-foot sailboat with two private cabins, a salon area for entertaining, a functional galley and a head with a shower. Though she knew nothing about boats, she felt with absolute surety that this one was incredibly expensive. She'd never been aboard without Ann so Kelly couldn't help hesitating.

She couldn't leave any stone unturned, a tiny voice reminded. Being thorough was essential.

Biting back the trepidation, she boarded the *Princess Ann,* instantly admiring its beauty.

Trent followed Kelly below deck, taking in the details of the magnificent vessel. Whatever Ann Jones, Annie Sutton or whoever, had been into, she'd made herself some hefty dough. The boat was loaded, from the gleaming mahogany to the stereo system. Hell, the place even had a galley kitchen better equipped than the one in his Chicago apartment.

"I'll only be a few minutes," she told him, then managed a smile that looked strained. "Make yourself at home."

He pretended fascination with the state-of-the-art stereo system and collection of CDs while she methodically went through every square inch of the luxurious boat. She checked each cabinet and drawer, twice. Her frustration level rose steadily with each dead end. Whatever she had hoped to find, she didn't.

She huffed a disgusted breath and closed her eyes wearily, then admitted defeat. "I'm sorry I kept you so long." She shrugged as if she didn't know what else to say. "We can go now."

He moved closer to her, took one of her hands in his in a gesture of comfort. "We'll find the answers. Maybe not today, but we'll find them. Don't beat yourself up."

Kelly looked deeply into those sea-blue eyes and wished she could understand what was happening between them…wished that she could tell him the truth. But then he'd go away. He wouldn't want to help her if he discovered that she had lied to him. His concern and desire was for Ann…not for her. She had to remember that. As much as she'd love to get lost in the fantasy, the truth was this fantasy belonged to another woman. That realization settled down on her like the *Titanic*'s anchor. However far she allowed this relationship to progress it would all be a lie. He would resent her later, might even grow to hate her.

She had to keep things on a platonic level. No matter how much she longed to get lost in those strong arms, it just wouldn't be right.

A thread of loneliness and regret worked its way through her as she realized the futility of it all. Ann was dead because of her. She owed it to her to see that her killer got what he deserved. She owed it to Ray as well. He'd been a good boss…a friend. Whatever steps she took, whatever moves she made, it all had to be for them.

She had to keep this man on her side. Had to see that he helped her accomplish that goal. No matter what was required of her on a personal level. She'd only just promised herself she wouldn't let this relationship progress beyond a certain point, but that might not be enough. Then and there she amended her earlier decision. She would do whatever it took to get this done. She wasn't blind, she'd seen the way he looked at her.

He wanted her.

She wanted him.

It was elementary.

THERE WAS SOMETHING entirely too solemn about Kelly as Trent drove back to the condo. She said little and seemed distracted. He made a stop at a drive-thru for sandwiches. She needed to eat, and sleep, to wipe that look of fatigue from her face. He wasn't sure if he could talk her into taking a nap while he was around…but he intended to give it a try.

When they were safely back at Ann's home and had shared lunch, he decided upon a suggestion he felt would intrigue her and quite possibly make her more receptive to his suggestions.

"I've been thinking about what you told me this morning," he began, garnering her attention as she tossed the remnants of their meal into the trash.

That worried gaze leveled on his. "And what conclusion did you reach?"

"I believe we need to take a look at the crime scene. See what we can find that the police might have missed. You know those men you hid from were looking for something in that office. The police don't know that. They might not look hard enough."

She appeared startled at first, then seemed to consider the possibility. "I would definitely like to get a good look around. I've thought about it a lot, in fact. But I didn't dare go back alone."

"It's decided then." He ushered her from the kitchen and toward the stairs. "You take a nap upstairs. I'll take one down here and tonight, under the cover of darkness, we'll see what we can find."

She hesitated. He couldn't be sure whether she wasn't comfortable with the sleeping arrangements or if she simply didn't want to wait until dark to go to Jarvis's office.

"We can both sleep upstairs…if you'd like."

A blast of need hit him hard but the uncertainty in her eyes quelled it.

"Not yet," he allowed, letting her off the hook. He wasn't certain of her motives, but he had a feeling it was about more than attraction. She badly needed a distraction, needed to be held.

They were both lying to each other right now. Not a good starting point for a relationship under normal conditions, definitely not considering the stress of this one. Not to mention that personal involvement was strictly off-limits for him. As much as he wanted her…as easy as it would be to make it happen with her so incredibly vulnerable right now…he didn't want it that way.

He kissed her cheek. "Get some sleep." He gestured to the living room. "I'll be right here when you wake up."

"SHE'S THERE ALL RIGHT."

Mac poured himself another drink and propped his feet up on his desk. He could drink all he wanted. Everyone else had already called it a day. The suite of Bureau offices in downtown Houston were officially closed. All except his. He still had a little business to finish up. "Hell, I saw her with *him*. They're up to something. You'd better tell that bastard to get back up here and get this thing squared away before it's too late."

He listened to the calm collected voice on the other end of the line. Stupid old goat. He took his own sweet time with everything. Hell, if it had been up to Mac, Jarvis would have been dead weeks ago. His stupid little assistant as well. And Mac would have done the job right the first time.

"Whatever you say. Just remember I warned you." He hung up and gulped down the glassful of Jim Beam in one long swallow. He made a satisfied sound and poured himself another. Let the fools screw this up even worse. He was covered. Nobody had a thing on him.

All he had to do was sit back and watch the rest of them wiggle like worms on hooks.

Chapter Eight

At 7:00 p.m. Trent hesitated outside the bedroom door before knocking. He hated to wake Kelly. She'd slept for several hours and that was good. She needed the rest. Hopefully she would be able to think more clearly, perhaps remember something important to the case. Witnesses always responded better if they felt calm and comfortable.

Three days of anxiety and fear had taken its toll on her. She had to be feeling the stress. She'd gone aboard that boat in a last-ditch effort to find something that would make sense of this all. He doubted she had any idea what she was looking for. She only knew that she had to look. He couldn't help feeling her angst…all too well. Not a good idea.

His cell phone vibrated in his pocket and Trent slipped away from the door without having knocked. He moved quickly down the stairs not daring to answer the call until he'd reached the entry hall, ensuring that his conversation would not be overheard.

"Tucker," he greeted.

"I got past the password," Heath told him without preamble.

There was a but, Trent sensed. "And?"

"The files are encrypted in some weird pattern. We've never seen anything like it. Mostly numbers."

Heath Murphy had the research department working overtime. A couple of those folks knew a thing or two about encryption.

"Is this something you can handle?" Trent couldn't be sure how much time they had. He hadn't been able to get through to Detective Hargrove all afternoon. That worried him. If word got out that Kelly had survived the hit on Jarvis's office everything would change. As things were, Trent could afford to play this little game of hidden identities, allowing Kelly to grow close to him and believe that he had no other agenda. However, if the stakes changed, that kind of deception could become a lethal liability.

"We're working on it," Heath allowed. "I'll give it twenty-four hours and if we've had no luck, we have a contact at N.S.A."

Trent knew Heath wouldn't waste the time if he wasn't relatively certain he could handle the project. He'd be back in touch with Trent well before the twenty-four hours were up.

"How about the Renaissance Corporation?"

The sound of Heath shuffling papers rattled across the line. "The corporation was set up one year ago by Ann Jones, but she's only listed as the CEO. The shareholders are listed as other, smaller companies. I'm still tracking those down."

That put Ann square in the middle of this game. He thought about the story Kelly had related to him this morning. She'd only survived the hit man because she'd been searching for something under the desk, hidden from view. Why had Ann been using the telephone at her desk at precisely that moment? What had Kelly been looking for on the floor? Who had dropped it? Was it an accident or a purposeful move?

Those were the kinds of questions he needed answers for. The only way he would learn those answers was to bond more fully with Kelly. Her invitation to join her upstairs this afternoon echoed inside his skull. As tempting as the offer was, he knew better than to cross that line. He had his own suspicions as to why she'd made the offer. She didn't seem the type to sleep with a stranger. But then, stress did bizarre things to people. His gut told him that she hoped the sex would somehow bind him to her more fully. Another naive concept. She really was an innocent in the way of these things. He wanted to protect that innocence.

"Let me know as soon as you can," Trent said in conclusion. "Thanks, Heath."

He scrubbed a hand over his face, his evening stubble scratching his palm. Who was Ann Jones really? She'd gone by Annie Sutton seven years ago when she'd been busted for drugs. But she'd dropped off the planet after the case was bargained down to a misdemeanor. What had she been doing all that time? And why had she suddenly shown up in Houston living in an exclusive neighborhood, driving a seventy-thousand-dollar car and partying weekends aboard a yacht?

More important, why had she befriended quiet, reserved, all alone in the world, Kelly Pruitt? Ann could certainly have worked her magic on Raymond Jarvis without the aid of his assistant.

A significant part of this puzzle was missing. Though he couldn't name it, he sensed it. The dead FBI agent fit perfectly into the scenario. He was a cover-up. Trent had no doubt on that score. Someone, quite possibly another agent, had set the guy up. There might not be a way to prove that theory, since there were no witnesses to what had taken place in that office. It seemed rather odd to Trent that the killer hadn't taken the money. Despite having been paid to terminate the people in that office, what criminal would walk away from twenty-five big ones in cash? Who was going to know? Unless it needed to be found in the G-man's pocket.

That, every instinct warned, was the answer. Agent Davis had taken the fall for someone else. But why Davis in particular? Why not someone from the local Bureau office?

To Trent's way of thinking, that Davis had come all the way from Dallas spelled something else entirely. Had Jarvis decided to go around the local office? Did he have reasonable motivation for that?

Trent needed to discuss these issues with Hargrove. Frustrated that he hadn't been able to reach the man, he punched in his number again. When he got no answer on his cell, he tried the office. He got the same song and dance all over again—Detective Hargrove was out on a case, would he like to leave a message?

Declining the offer, Trent punched the end button and entered the senator's private number next. Maybe he knew where the hell Hargrove was.

"Hello."

Tension went through Trent. There was a tremor in the senator's voice. "Senator, this is Trent Tucker."

"I was just going to call you," the senator began, the tremor still present, "I've received some unsettling news."

The hair on the back of Trent's neck stood on end. "What kind of news?"

"The Houston Bureau office has taken Detective Hargrove into custody for questioning. They won't let me speak to him and they refuse to answer any of my questions. How can they do that, Mr. Tucker?"

Trent repressed the anticipation that seared through him, careful to keep his tone even, his voice reassuring. "There's only one reason they would do that, Senator," he explained. "Hargrove must have stumbled on to some part of an ongoing investigation being conducted by the feds. This kind of interrogation is routine. The fact that they won't give you any information is more telling than you realize. Hargrove has uncovered something that could blow their case. They'll keep him in lockdown until they feel the threat has passed."

"How can I be sure they aren't covering up something?" he urged. "They've done this before. I'm just certain it has to do with the drug cartel."

Trent could understand his concern, but he was

overreacting. "Senator, there may very well be someone in the Houston office who isn't on the up and up. But the idea that everyone on the federal payroll in that district is on the take is highly unlikely. They may be conducting their own internal affairs investigation in conjunction with this case. We can't know for sure. Staying calm right now is the best strategy." The last thing he needed was for the senator to blast the FBI with news that he'd hired a private firm to look into the situation. Trent could only hope that Hargrove would cover for him.

But Trent didn't know the detective well enough to be able to count on that kind of alliance. The reality was that he was running out of time. If Hargrove spilled his guts about Trent's participation in this case, the feds would be tracking him down. Kelly would be taken into custody and then there was no way to ensure how things would go from there.

And that wasn't even considering what steps the hit man would take when he learned of Kelly's survival and her association with Trent.

They had to move fast.

He ended the call with the senator and turned back toward the stairs to wake sleeping beauty.

But she was already up.

Standing on the landing staring down at him with a look of worried confusion on her face.

He could only guess at how long she'd been listening to his conversation.

"We should get going," he suggested, hoping she'd heard only the final moments of the exchange.

She nodded. "Just let me get a jacket."

He had to suppress the need to fly up the stairs and see that she wasn't trying to escape out the bedroom window. But he held his ground, gave her the benefit of the doubt. If he made a preemptive move right now that would tip the scales in the wrong direction. He had to give the illusion that all was as it should be. That nothing she had heard could possibly mean what she might fear it did.

More lies.

More deception.

But if it kept her alive and got the case solved, it was a good thing, right?

KELLY SLIPPED ON the black velvet jacket that matched the slacks she'd taken from Ann's closet. She'd selected a black shell as well. If the plan was to enter the office at dark she wanted to blend into the night. To that end she'd fastened her hair into a bun, then wound and tied a black scarf around it. Her blond bangs managed to wiggle free but she could live with that.

As she moved back toward the bedroom door she hesitated, the final words of Trent's telephone conversation replaying in her mind. *I'll keep you informed, Senator. I've got everything under control.*

What senator? What did Trent have under control?

To some degree she wasn't worried. What would a senator have to do with her? But then, a tiny voice kept reminding her that she really didn't know this man. As nice as he seemed, as much as he appeared to want to help her, he was still a stranger. Never in a million years would she recommend her current course of action to anyone. But her situation was extreme, calling for drastic measures.

But would those drastic measures get her killed?

Was death imminent in spite of all that she'd attempted to prevent it? Would solving this case matter?

And what had possessed her to be so forward as to ask him to sleep upstairs? With her! She had to be losing it.

All those questions whirled inside her head, making her dizzy with worry and confusion.

She shook off the sensations and squared her shoulders. By God, she was not going to take this lying down. Whether she accomplished anything or not, she had to try. She had to do it for her friends…for herself.

Trent Tucker was all she had.

Maybe she'd gamble and lose, but at least she was in the game.

Trent waited at the front door as she descended the stairs. He was right, the few hours of sleep had worked wonders. She felt immensely better.

His gaze locked with hers and she saw the reassurance there. Whatever his agenda, if he even had one, he would help her. She could trust him. So what if he was keeping a thing or two to himself, so was she.

Like the disk and the fact that she was not Ann Jones.

Who was to say who was deceiving whom here?

Too complicated, she decided, shoving the thought away.

THE NIGHT WAS CLEAR. A thousand stars twinkled overhead, reminding her that life truly did go on. She might never get her old life back, but she was alive and for the moment that mattered a great deal.

She studied the man behind the wheel in the dim glow from the dash. There was a grimness about him tonight that she hadn't seen before. Not that she had seen that much of him. They'd barely known each other twenty-four hours. Okay, so he didn't actually know her at all. She was complicating things again. Pushing the details away, she focused on the physical. What she could see…what she knew.

There was a kindness about Trent Tucker. She guessed his age at thirty, hadn't dared ask since that would only lead to questions about her and more lies. The fine lines, invisible in this low lighting but easily seen beneath the Texas sun's glare, spoke of some amount of world-weariness. She could imagine that he'd either suffered some personal loss or maybe the cases he'd worked had left their mark on his handsome face.

She picked up the hat that spent more time on the seat of the truck than on his head and turned it over in her hands. She did so love cowboys. On the ranch growing up she'd watched her father ride and rope, even helped out in a little branding from time to time. She remembered the feel of his leather chaps and the sound they made when he walked.

A smile tugged at her lips as she recalled him winking at her in the morning before settling his hat on his head and mounting his horse. He'd loved his life…had loved his family, too much it seemed. He'd followed her mother to the grave far too quickly for Kelly. She'd been left all alone with a big old ranch she couldn't bear to oversee and no one in the world to hold her when she felt afraid or to wink at her as the day began to let her know that all was right in the world.

She blinked back the tears that threatened and kicked herself for allowing the self-pity session. She'd managed on her own and though she might never find the cowboy of her dreams, she would be okay.

Life wasn't always fair. She had to make the best of it.

Trent parked about two blocks from the office. Kelly focused on her surroundings. She walked this way most every afternoon to make a delivery to the post office. She enjoyed the walk, knew the area.

''I'd like to check things out first,'' Trent told her quietly. ''You stay here and I'll come back for you.''

She surveyed the dark street and buildings. ''I think I'd rather go with you.'' She might know the area well in the light of day, but right now it looked pretty ominous.

''All right, but stay behind me.''

She nodded her understanding, enjoying again the idea of being protected.

He picked up a small duffel-like bag and got out of the truck. By the time he moved around to her side of the vehicle she was already on the sidewalk.

She couldn't help glancing at the bag in his hand again and wondering what it contained. Seeming to read her mind yet again, he explained, "Flashlights, tools we might need."

Thankful he'd had the foresight to come prepared, she followed the path he made. He weaved around and behind buildings, choosing the darkest recesses for their journey, including a maze of overgrown shrubbery. She understood the necessity but that didn't make her like it. She'd always been just the tiniest bit afraid of the dark.

Slowly they made their way to the back of the office. Trent used a tool from the bag on the lock. She gasped when the door opened as easily as if he'd possessed a key.

"Even the cops learn how to negotiate a locked door," he whispered.

"I'm not sure I want to know what else they taught you," she murmured teasingly as he passed her a flashlight.

She didn't have to see him smile to know he had, she heard it in his voice. "How am I supposed to impress you otherwise?"

Hesitating at the door, her eyes seeking his in the darkness, she heard herself ask, "Are you trying to impress me?" She hadn't meant to ask the question, it simply popped out.

He took her hand and tugged her inside, allowing the door to close, leaving them in an even inkier darkness. "I think I must be," he said in answer to her question.

For a space in time she couldn't make herself move past that moment. She wanted to hang on with both hands and pretend everything else away. But in the next second the lingering smell of death hit her nostrils and all other thoughts vanished in its wake.

"I'll walk you through what happened," she said gravely as she forced herself forward. Falling for this guy wasn't going to bring her friends' murderer to justice.

Taking her time, careful not to leave anything out, she walked him through last Friday evening from the moment Ann asked to use the phone, without, of course, giving her identity away.

He crouched down behind her desk and surveyed the area with his flashlight. She shivered at the chalk outline on the floor of where her friend had fallen.

"What were you looking for under here?"

"A disk," she said before she thought. "A music CD actually," she amended quickly. "It fell off the desk and then An—she accidentally bumped it with her shoe, sending it sliding across the tile and under the desk."

Trent had heard that story twice already and it didn't make sense still. He'd viewed the clothes the victims had been wearing. Ann Jones had worn pointed toe, high-heel shoes. In order for her to have kicked the CD under the desk rather than merely stepping on it, she would have had to angle her foot just right since the toe of her shoe turned up slightly. He flattened his lips in a grim line. That's what had been bothering him about that scenario. He'd known it didn't fit somehow but hadn't been able to pursue the subject with Kelly without rousing her suspicions.

"So you crawled under here to retrieve it and that's when the killer came in."

"That's right."

Perfect timing. Trent didn't believe in coincidences. Not that they didn't occur on rare occasions, but rare was the key word.

He stood, considered the options. He'd been over this place thoroughly with Hargrove, but she didn't know that. "Well, let's see what we can find."

Who knew? Maybe she would find something or notice something he hadn't.

More than an hour later he had to give her credit. She was thorough and methodical.

While she surveyed Jarvis's office once more, Trent propped his hip against the corner of the man's desk and thumbed through his Rolodex. He and Hargrove had gone through it, matching names with files. There were a few business contact numbers, all checked out. His girlfriend. That reminded Trent, he needed to ask Heath how the search for the girlfriend was going. Hargrove was supposed to have gotten back to him on that. But the detective was indisposed at the moment.

Trent frowned and backed up a card. There was a number written on the back of the last card he'd looked at. He rotated the Rolodex one-eighty and started flipping through it from the backside. He came across at least a dozen numbers written on the backs of cards. On the front side was a client's name, address and telephone number, but on the back a mere six digit number with no notation as to what it represented.

"Do you know what these numbers are?" Trent

asked as Kelly closed the doors to her former boss's credenza.

She moved up next to him, the feel of her so close, making his gut clench and his respiration quicken.

"Oh those. They're designation numbers for his online files."

"What do you mean?"

"I don't know that much about the cyber world, but Ray wanted to be able to access his files from home or anywhere else via the Internet. So he downloaded the information onto a secure site but instead of using names and other sensitive client info, he tagged each one with a number that would distinguish who the client was. He memorized the numbers and kept a hard copy here." She indicated the Rolodex.

"So the number on the back of the card matches the client on the front."

She shook her head. "No, he thought that'd be too easy. He went in reverse alphabetical order. The last number in the Rolodex goes with the first client in the alphabet."

Trent considered the steps Jarvis had taken and decided there was nothing questionable about his method. Security on the Internet was a tricky balance, these sorts of measures were understandable, however primitive.

"Maybe we should take this with us," he suggested.

"Could be useful," she agreed.

Trent opened his duffel and placed the Rolodex inside. "Anything else around here you think we might need?"

She sighed and considered the question for a bit. "I don't think so. We can access the files online."

"Jarvis didn't keep any disks that might prove beneficial?"

Even in the dim light reflected from where the beam of his flashlight bounced off the desk, he could easily make out the startled look on her face. She'd actually given herself away moments ago when she'd spoken so candidly about how *Ray* added his files to the Internet. She'd forgotten to call him Mr. Jarvis and hadn't considered that she was telling too much. Why would Ann Jones know so much about Jarvis's filing system? The slip about the disk, which she'd assured him meant music CD, confirmed his suspicions that the disk he'd found in the laptop at Ann's town house carried some significance to the case.

"No...not that I know of," she stammered in answer to his question about disks. "I'm sure they're all filed away with the appropriate client's account information."

"I guess we should get out of here then." He picked up his bag and moved the beam of his light toward the door leading to the corridor.

The flashlights were turned off and deposited back into the bag before they exited via the rear of the building. The moon and streetlamps would provide sufficient light for their return journey to the truck.

Just as they reached the end of the office complex a dark sedan pulled into the parking lot.

Trent's senses went on high alert. He stilled, ensuring Kelly was fully behind him.

"You take the back," a male voice called out as four men emerged from the vehicle.

All four wore black ski masks and combat attire.

Behind him Kelly gasped.

He faced her and pressed a finger to his lips. He shouldn't have brought her here...should have anticipated the danger. But it was too late now.

Moving as stealthily as possible with her clinging to him, he ushered her into the overgrown shrubbery that flanked the end of the building and led into the parking area.

Thankfully they were both wearing dark colored clothing. He sank into the evergreen shrubs, drawing her against his chest and allowing the thick limbs to drape in front of them, camouflaging their position.

Two men came around behind the building from the alleyway that connected this office with the next one, the orthodontist's clinic. They surveyed the back alley and quickly shimmied the door open in much the same manner as Trent had. Once inside they closed the door behind them.

For several minutes Trent listened for the other two, finally concluding that they had entered the building via the front.

He leaned close to Kelly's ear and whispered, "I'm going to turn around and dig my way through this shrubbery. Stay close to my back."

She nodded, her fingers gripping his arms like vises.

As he soundlessly wove his way through the overgrown mass of evergreens and cedar shrubs, the one thing that kept reverberating in his head was thank God Jarvis had never bothered with a landscaping service.

Chapter Nine

Not until they were in the truck and headed back to Galveston did Kelly breathe easy again. She closed her eyes and leaned back against the seat and concentrated on slowing her respiration and the pounding of her heart.

She kept hearing the voices from that evening. The one man ordering the others to do his bidding—to tear the office apart and yet to put everything back as they'd found it. Now and then she'd heard one of the others speak.

Her eyes flew open. "It was them."

Trent glanced at her. "From that night?"

She nodded and struggled for the next breath. "Not…him, but the others. I recognized the way they dressed, like SWAT personnel. Well, except I didn't see the masks. But that didn't mean it was the same guys until I remembered that voice. Not the murderer's voice, but one of the others," she repeated. "Why would they come back again? They got what they wanted."

She snapped her mouth shut and prayed he would

believe her comment referred to the murders. Holding her breath until he spoke again, his next words shot down any hope she'd had that her slip would go unnoticed.

"What was it they wanted?"

She cursed herself silently and frantically thought of some way to clarify what she'd meant without telling him the truth.

"I thought you trusted me," he murmured, his voice softly intriguing.

She did trust him, didn't she? But, did she trust him that much? Could she take that kind of risk? She shook her head. What difference did it make? Keeping up with all these lies was only making things more complicated. Complicated was not good.

Telling him about the disk wouldn't hurt. She sure as heck hadn't been able to find her way around the password. Maybe he could.

"I heard the killer tell whoever he called on his cell phone that he had the disk."

"What disk?" Trent prodded, his deep, gentle voice tugging away at her resolve, urging her to tell him the rest.

"Okay." She had to do this in a way that wouldn't give away who she really was. That was the one thing she intended to keep to herself. "Ray gave his…Kelly a disk before he took that client—the FBI agent—into his office. Told her to take it home with her and keep it safe. He stressed that she shouldn't keep it at the office and that she might need it sometime." A heavy breath slipped between her lips as she recalled the look on Ray's face as he urged her to heed his words.

"That's what I was retrieving under the desk when the killer came in. An—Kelly knocked it onto the floor and I was getting it for...her." God, she had to keep the names straight. "I'm assuming that the disk is a duplicate of the one the killer said he had. Maybe Ray wanted backup evidence. I don't know."

"You have the disk then?" Trent glanced at her again, his expression a blank mask.

That he so carefully concealed his reaction to this news made her uneasy. "Yes. I...it's in the laptop."

The one she'd left unattended on more than one occasion in the past two days.

Trent apparently had the same thought because he sped up as if every second mattered.

She sagged back into the seat and peered out the window at the dark landscape whizzing by. It would be so much simpler if she could just tell him the rest. Tell him everything.

But she couldn't...not yet. It didn't make sense...she trusted him on so many levels already, but telling him her real name seemed too much. As Ann she was anonymous to an extent.

Trent circled the block twice before he parked along the curb on the street one block down and behind Ann's home. "What're you doing?" He was making her feel uneasy again. As if he knew something she didn't, and whatever it was it wasn't good.

"Just making sure that we don't have any company," he told her, but the answer did little to ease her anxiety.

He got out and scanned left to right as he moved around to her side of the truck. "Stay behind me."

She'd gotten used to his orders so she didn't question him. She supposed he'd been around cops enough to know when to use caution. Something she should learn if she intended to survive this fugitive gig.

They moved between the houses, weaving between bushes and trees much as they had when they'd gone to the office. His tactics had worked then, she had no reason to doubt him now. When they reached Ann's condo he took the key from her and unlocked the front door. Before he opened the door he hesitated long enough to draw a weapon from beneath his jacket.

Her eyes widened and her mouth dropped open. What the hell? Since when did reporters carry guns?

Too startled to protest, she followed him inside the dark house. She almost jumped out of her skin when Felix flew out the door around her. She pressed her hand to her chest and fought to steady herself.

"Don't move," Trent told her, ushering her against the wall near the door.

Utterly stunned, she stood like a statue as he crept through the darkness checking room after room. Did he suspect someone was in the house? Had he seen something she hadn't? Why the hell had he left her standing by the door in this damned corner?

The answer dawned on her no sooner than the question crossed her mind. Where she stood was the darkest corner of the entry hall. If someone were in the house and came rushing toward the door he would never see her. The same would hold true if an intruder entered the house while Trent checked things out. She was well hidden in this spot.

If he wasn't on the up and up, he certainly wouldn't care what happened to her. Maybe she could tell him the whole truth? Get this weight off her shoulders. It wasn't like the police didn't know by now. If she took the time to watch the news she'd probably find her face plastered over the airwaves instructing anyone who saw her to call the police.

She rubbed her eyes and worked diligently to block the thoughts. Thinking that way wasn't going to help, the only purpose it served was to upset her. She didn't need to deal with any additional crap. Be smart, she told herself, don't think at all.

The entry hall light came on and Trent approached her. "It's all right. The house is clear."

"Did you have reason to believe it wasn't?" She had to know. She hadn't seen any reason to consider otherwise.

"Just a precaution," he told her.

She nodded, too weary to argue the point any further. The disk. She should check to make sure the disk was still in the laptop.

Without explanation she hurried to Ann's office and pressed the eject button for the disk drive. Nothing happened. Dread roiling inside her, she pushed it again.

"It's gone," Trent told her as he leaned against the doorframe. "I already checked."

Someone had been here. Someone who knew she'd survived. "We have to get out of here," she murmured, her gaze locking with his. "If they know I've got the disk—"

The sound of breaking glass cut off the rest of her words.

The next thing she knew Trent was tugging her behind him as he zigzagged through the house. Glass kept breaking but there was no sound of gunfire.

"What's happening?" She stayed close behind him, his left hand wrapped fully around her right.

"They're using silencers."

Like they had at the office that night, she realized. Those little hissing pops were all she'd heard. Since the shots were coming from outside all she could hear now was the glass breaking.

It was those same men. She didn't have to see them to know. They knew she was alive and they intended to remedy that situation.

They wanted her dead.

Trent doubled back to the entry hall and rushed up the stairs with Kelly right behind him. Thankfully she didn't ask any questions, just followed his lead. Their escape options were limited. Going out the front or back doors would be suicide.

That left only the upstairs windows. The condos were connected. The roofs high pitched with numerous architectural embellishments to set them apart visually. That would work, he decided.

But the only window that overlooked the roof was the one in the master bath. With gable ends facing the front and back yards and the darkness for cover, they weren't likely to be seen from the ground.

It took several hard shoves to free the rarely opened

window. "Climb out onto the roof," he told her. "I'll be right behind you."

She stared at him. Her eyes wide with fear and uncertainty. He could see the emotions clearly despite the dim glow of the night-light. Or maybe he sensed her emotions. "Hurry," he urged.

Footsteps poured into the entry hall downstairs. It wouldn't be long until they were pounding up the stairs.

She blinked as if coming out of a haze and then scrambled over the commode to get out the window. He pushed through next, lowering the window behind him.

"Come on." He gripped her right hand tightly as he moved to the next roof.

The shingles were slick with the dampness of the night but still rough textured enough to provide traction.

If they were really lucky their pursuers would think they'd managed to escape from a window downstairs and rush out into the yard looking for them.

But they weren't going to be that lucky.

The sound of boot heels scraping against the asphalt shingles behind them warned Trent that he had to make a decision now.

He moved to the next roof, all but dragging Kelly behind him. Moving far faster than he would have preferred he slid down to the lower level roof spanning the condo's rear patio. An option the owners had likely added since none of the other condos had covered patios.

Barely stopping his downward descent before going over the edge, he pulled Kelly close and whispered in her ear, "I'm going to jump. As soon as I'm on my feet, jump into my arms."

She shook her head. "I can't jump!" She leaned toward the edge. "It's too far."

He took her by the shoulders and shook her gently. "They're right behind us. There's no time to argue."

Then he jumped.

Kelly watched him land on his feet then roll with the impact of hitting the ground.

He was up in an instant. His arms outstretched toward her.

She couldn't do it.

No way.

She shook her head.

He gestured wildly for her to jump not daring to call out to her.

Fear tightened around her throat and she started to shake.

She couldn't do this.

A pop hissed past her head like a bee buzzing through the air. Trent jumped to one side.

She blinked.

What…

He waved to her, the movements even more frantic.

Another muffled pop.

He jerked to the side almost stumbling.

Gunshots!

The realization struck her like lightning and in that same instant she jumped.

She hit the ground hard. Feet first…hands and

knees...then onto her shoulder. Her head slammed against the grass.

The world spun when she opened her eyes.

Moving.

He was dragging her under the patio.

Glass shattered.

Sirens blared.

That was the last thing Kelly heard.

TRENT STOOD beneath the hot spray of the shower and reveled in the feel of it sluicing over his tired muscles. His left shoulder was pretty banged up but nothing was broken. He had a few scratches but he'd live.

Kelly was still out, but he'd checked on her right before getting into the shower. She was fine. No concussion. He figured she'd gone unconscious more from the fear than from hitting the ground.

Thank God for security systems. Knowing that the patio roof was the only cover they had from the shooter and that his friends would likely come barreling through the adjoining yards at any moment, he'd slung that wrought-iron chair through the patio doors in hopes of waking the owners so they'd call the police. The sirens from the home security system had been even better. Their pursuers had run like hell.

During the fray that followed as the inhabitants of one home after the other had hurried out to see what was going on, he'd thrown Kelly over his good shoulder and double timed it to his truck. He'd driven until he found a hotel off the beaten path and he'd gotten a room under an alias.

Once he'd checked Kelly out thoroughly and talked her through the hysteria she'd suffered when she'd come to, he'd ordered some food from a nearby restaurant that delivered. But she'd fallen back to sleep before the food arrived. Trent had decided to wait until she was ready to eat to dig in himself. He needed a shower anyway.

He lathered his hair and body, rinsing quickly and climbing out. He didn't want her out of his sight any longer than necessary. She might just run again. Not that he could blame her. Escaping hit men a second time was enough to make anyone wary of risking a third confrontation.

Mopping the towel over his body, he made quick work of drying. Without bothering to shave, he slung the towel around his waist and went to check on her again. He didn't like that she'd gone back to sleep again so quickly. He supposed it could be her way of escaping a harsh reality, but still, he didn't like it. He'd had enough emergency medical training to know she displayed no symptoms of a head injury. She had no broken bones or other visible injuries. But shock was another story. Mental trauma could bring that on as easily as physical injury.

To his surprise she was sitting in the middle of the bed devouring a two-portion container of fried rice.

Kelly looked up at the sound of Trent coming out of the bathroom and the fork stalled halfway to her open mouth. The weight of the rice was suddenly too much and her hand sank to the mattress, thankfully with the box of rice in the upright position.

HIS SKIN was still damp from his shower. He'd dried off, but only haphazardly. His hair was wet and tousled, streaks of the brown stuff plastered to his brow. The stubble on his chin made him look...dangerous. But it was the bare masculine terrain of that gorgeous torso that derailed all rational thought processes.

Broad, broad shoulders. A mile wide chest that narrowed into a lean, taut abdomen. The towel hung precariously on those slim hips, covering what were surely powerful thighs but revealing muscled calves and long, well-formed feet.

The image made her want to take her clothes off. Made her want to scale that mountain of a man and forget everything else that had happened.

She blinked. Shifted her gaze to the rice in her hand. Shock, she mused. That's all it could be. She'd been shot at, twice, hidden in a ventilation duct, jumped off a building. She had every right to be delirious. She'd all but asked him to have sex with her already.

"I'm sorry. I thought you were still asleep."

She held up the hand with the fork. "It's okay." She blinked repeatedly to dispel the amazing image burned into her retinas. "I shouldn't have stared."

He grabbed his jeans and disappeared into the bathroom once more. She sat stock still, listening to the sound of soft denim rasping against bare skin as he tugged on his jeans. The glide of metal on metal hailed the zipping of his fly. Seconds later he appeared again, those well-worn jeans hugging his strong body like a second skin.

Forcing her attention back to the rice she found that her appetite had fled for parts unknown. Determined to at least look like his body hadn't affected her so much, she dug back into the rice.

He pulled a container of rice from one of the bags and proceeded to chow down using the chopsticks. She rolled her eyes. She should have known. A guy as perfect as him would know how to use any kind of tool. She shivered at the thought of what else he was probably quite adept at.

"Does your head hurt?" he asked between bites.

"Just a little. Mainly my hands and knees are sore." She remembered landing on her feet, but the impact had flung her down onto her hands and knees and then on her side. But her fall hadn't broken the skin or given her any lumps. Her head had hit the ground hard enough to jar her equilibrium, but she felt fine now.

"That's good."

They ate in silence for a while. She thought about the way he'd held her in those strong arms when she'd awakened in this bed, frightened and disoriented. He'd held her close to that awesome chest, whispered soothingly in her ear. Over and over. He'd washed her face with cool water, and had checked her arms, legs and any other part of her body he deemed necessary for injury. She remembered him ordering the food but she'd been too tired to stay awake. She'd had to sleep.

When she'd opened her eyes once more she'd been ravenous. He was in the shower so she'd dug in. She sipped her cola now and studied him covertly.

She absently wondered if she'd fallen way short of the expectations he'd had for the Juliet he'd been courting via the Internet. He'd certainly turned down her invitation this afternoon readily enough. To be honest, she was glad he had. She gave her head a little shake. She didn't know what she'd been thinking. Maybe that she could trust him more if there was a physical connection. Well that was just her inexperience speaking. Sex didn't make guys trust a girl more, or vice versa. She traced the planes and contours of that awesome chest with her eyes. It had been a long time since she'd been with a man. Not that she'd had that many relationships. Three, if you counted the one that only lasted a couple of weeks and didn't include sex.

She let go a heavy breath. She was young. It wasn't like she didn't have time.

The events of the past few days flashed through her mind and instantly had her revising that last statement. Okay, maybe she didn't have plenty of time.

Her gaze went to Trent once more. But hot, raw sex with the perfect man wasn't the answer to her current dilemma.

"What do we do now?" she ventured, uncertain if she was really ready to know the answer to that question.

His gaze collided with hers and heat sizzled along every nerve ending in her body then sank all the way to her bones, turning them to mush. How she managed to keep breathing was a complete mystery to her.

"We take it easy until morning. It's late, we're both tired. We can figure out something in the morning."

Sounded reasonable to her. The second bed in the

room dragged her attention in that direction. They would be in separate beds...but only a few feet apart. She chewed her lower lip to quench the fire starting up inside her again. Every time she thought about how he'd held her against him in those bushes at the office she couldn't help remembering the hard contours of his body. Even in the midst of a life-and-death situation she'd felt a masculine bulge that made her shiver with need.

She swallowed hard and thought about the way he'd held on to her hand so tight as they scaled roof after roof. Or the feel of his hands moving over her body as he checked her for injury. If she let her mind dwell on how he'd held her, well, she'd simply lose control and attack him.

It was the stress, she told herself. Stress, shock, vulnerability, the fear of dying. That's all it was.

She didn't generally sit around thinking about sex.

But then she didn't usually spend all her time running from killers, either.

She climbed off the bed and set the half-empty box of rice on the table. If she couldn't jump his bones then she'd just eat something else to distract herself. There were several more containers. Cashew chicken, some sort of spicy beef, mixed vegetables. Paper plates had been provided, so she dug a helping from each container, dumped the food onto the plate and decided that should do the trick.

If this didn't keep her distracted, nothing would.

In spite of her best intentions she sneaked a peek from the corner of her eye.

He was looking directly at her.

She jumped.

Almost dropped her plate.

He stood abruptly and set his food aside. ''I'm going out for a while.''

She watched him stride across the room, barefoot, shirtless, her mouth gaping open like a fool's.

''Wait!'' she managed to croak as soon as she'd stopped admiring his butt.

He hesitated at the door, giving her time to catch up with him. ''Where are you going?''

If the heat in his eyes was any indication of the fire inside him he was on his way to spontaneous combustion just as she was.

''You want the truth or do you want me to make something up?'' he asked bluntly, his tone hard, gritty, too damned sexy.

''The...truth of course.''

He looked so deeply into her eyes that she couldn't breath, couldn't move, couldn't do anything but stare back at him, knowing full well that the longing inside her was reflected in her eyes for him to see.

''I need some space before I do something we'll both regret.''

''But I...'' She tried to come up with a plausible excuse for her own behavior, which had, apparently, set off his. But she couldn't think of anything to say, she could only look at him. As if to emphasize her lack of control, her gaze swept down the length of him and back up to that incredible face. She suddenly felt certain she had a fever.

''You have to stop looking at me that way,'' he

murmured, his face closer somehow or maybe it was her imagination. "I can't...not react."

She blinked in an attempt to clear the haze of pure lust from her brain but it didn't work. "I'm sorry," she said breathlessly. "It's just that I've never known anyone like you." Her gaze dropped to that massive chest once more. "You're so strong...and so..." Before she could stop herself she'd touched him. Flattened her palm against his chest which stole any breath she'd had left in her lungs.

He took her chin between his thumb and forefinger and lifted her face up to his. "You're not making this easy," he murmured softly, his tone deadly.

It should have scared the hell out of her, but it didn't. She just kept staring at his mouth, mesmerized by the way his lips moved. And then he groaned like a trapped animal. That devastating mouth swooped down on hers and he kissed her like she had never been kissed before. There was no gentleness this time...no tender brushing of lips. This was passion personified. Red-hot lust sizzling down to its most basic form.

When he drew back she staggered drunkenly.

He steadied her. "I'll be back. Don't leave the room."

And then he was gone.

Leaving her to burn up all by herself.

Chapter Ten

Trent walked for a good fifteen minutes before he'd calmed down. He just didn't get this total overreaction his entire system kept having to the woman. He'd analyzed the attraction six ways to Sunday and still it made no sense.

He just couldn't get his head on straight where she was concerned. She'd pushed some button he hadn't known existed. If he believed that there was one certain woman for every man he might just be inclined to think that she was the one. But he didn't put stock in any such nonsense.

He shook off the lingering lust. Damn, he'd never had this much trouble with control before. A couple more laps around the motel building and he was good to go.

Calm as the proverbial cucumber. And freezing his ass off. He'd left the room without a shirt or a jacket. Hell he was even barefoot. But the infusing cold had done its job. His body was back under control.

He fished his cell phone from his pocket and punched in the number for Heath. It was late but

Heath wouldn't mind. He expected calls at all hours of the night. When he reached his truck he unlocked it and sat down behind the wheel. He started to crank the engine and turn on the heat but that would defeat the purpose of this little exercise in discipline.

"Murphy," rasped across the line.

"I didn't get you up, did I?"

"It's cool. I haven't been in bed long. What's up? We haven't figured out the code yet if that's why you're calling. We're getting close though."

Trent reached for his duffel. "I hope so. It looks like the other side has a copy now, too. If they didn't already." He hated like hell that they'd gotten to the laptop and found the disk. But he hadn't been able to hide it without giving himself away to Kelly. "I might have something that will help." He set the Rolodex where he could access it, then switched on the interior light. "I'm going to give you about a dozen names with a coordinating number. The numbers are supposed to somehow tie into the accounts."

"Let me get to my desk," Heath muttered.

Trent could hear him moving around, cursing as he bumped into something in his path.

"Have you watched the news tonight?" he asked as he rifled through pages, probably in a notebook.

"Did I miss something?"

"The senator called and wanted to know if I knew anything about the fire at the Jarvis firm and if I'd heard anything from you? He also mentioned that the feds were posting Kelly Pruitt's photo on their Web site as well as local news channels asking anyone who's seen her to call in."

Trent swore. Just what they needed. As far as the fire was concerned there hadn't been anything useful to the investigation in that office. He thought about the men who'd shown up tonight at the office as he and Kelly had been leaving. "They're covering their tracks." A little late, but getting to it. He'd wondered why they hadn't simply burned the place down when the murders were committed. The dead agent with the bribe in his pocket had to be extremely important for them to risk allowing evidence to be found. As far as Kelly's identity, he imagined that Hargrove had caved and spilled his guts.

"Yeah, guess they are. According to the senator there's nothing left of the office complex." He yawned noisily. "Okay, shoot with the names and numbers."

Trent called off the names in alphabetical order, then turned the Rolodex around and recited the co-ordinating numbers.

"I'll get on this first thing in the a.m."

"Call the senator for me," Trent told him. "Let him know that my investigation is on track. Don't give him any information on my location. It's not that I don't trust him, but he may trust someone that he shouldn't."

"Will do."

"Hey," Trent remembered before hanging up, "you find anything on Jarvis's missing girlfriend yet? Darlene Whitehead?"

"I've got a former New Orleans cop checking for me. He thinks Whitehead might be a married name.

I'll give him a nudge, too. See if I can light a fire under him.''

"Let me know as soon as you have anything.''

Trent ended the call, turned off the interior light in his truck and considered whether or not Kelly would be asleep by now. He really needed some distance but couldn't risk getting a separate room. He felt reasonably certain they were safe for the moment, but she could decide to run. Especially if she got a glimpse of the latest news reports.

Heaving a frustrated groan, Trent snagged the duffel and locked up his truck. No point putting off the inevitable. He crossed the lot to their room. Downstairs and with the door facing the parking lot they could get to the truck in a hurry if need be. He slid the keycard into the lock and pushed the door open.

The television was on, but her eyes were closed. Good. He flipped the secondary lock into place and put the chain on for good measure. His body shivered as the warm air enveloped him. He cursed himself for the fool he was. The smell of leftover Chinese hung in the air like a friend who'd overstayed his welcome.

Trent set the duffel on a chair and busied himself clearing away the remains of their dinner. He bagged the leftovers and carried the sack to a trashcan he'd noticed next to the ice machine beneath the stairs leading to the upper floor.

When he returned to the room Kelly was sitting in the middle of the bed her gaze glued to the television screen. She quickly turned it off. If she'd been watching the news she now knew that her face was plastered all over the place. Dammit, he'd needed a little more time before that happened. But as long as she didn't know he knew, things could remain status quo.

He shivered again and resisted the urge to kick himself. The temperature outside had dropped considerably. What damn fool walked around half-naked in the middle of a winter's night? Even in Texas January nights could be brutal.

Kelly glanced up at him, careful not to look directly into his eyes. "Mr. Jarvis's office burned down."

"I heard." He jerked his head toward the door. "On the radio." He kept the other to himself, only now rolling the full ramifications over in his head. Anyone who saw her was to call the FBI. That figured. They'd taken the case from the local cops. Things would be done their way now, which was not a good thing for Kelly. Though Trent felt certain they would eventually clear her of wrongdoing, this could drag on and on, not to mention they could get her killed. They had to know that the killer would see the broadcast.

His eyes narrowed as he turned the concept over again. Maybe that's what they wanted. The killer on her tail. If they suspected that she had herself a protector who knew the ropes of investigation, they might just be running that news flash to bait the killer.

Surely the Bureau's need to get this guy wouldn't go as far as risking the life of an innocent civilian or two. He'd have to try and keep her out of sight from this point on. Time wasn't on his side. He sure as hell hoped Heath found what they needed in those damned files.

"What do we do now?"

She huddled beneath the covers, the spread pulled up to her chin. He noticed then that she was shaking. As much as he knew it would cost him, he couldn't deny her the comfort she needed. As worried and frightened as she was, she still wasn't ready to tell him the whole truth. To an extent he understood. She needed reassuring…maybe then she'd come clean with him.

Trent sat down next to her and put his arm around her shoulders. God she was warm and he was still freezing. "Everything's going to be fine. I'm not going to let anything happen to you." She smelled so good. Soft and sweet and womanly. He pushed that line of thinking away. "We didn't find anything in the office anyway. Those men probably didn't, either, before they burned it down."

Confusion lined her delicate brow. "Why would you take a risk like this? To keep me safe, I mean. You don't even know me."

Oh, but he did. She just didn't know that part. A stab of guilt sliced through him, but he ignored it. He shrugged, buying time while he dredged his weary brain for a workable response. "I guess I can't turn my back on a challenge." He smiled down at her then. "Besides, I've kind of gotten attached to you."

That was truer than it needed to be.

She glanced at his jacket and the weapon still safely tucked in his shoulder holster lying next to it. "Why do you carry a gun?"

He'd hoped that little detail had slipped under her radar. Luck just wasn't on his side tonight. "I decided it was necessary a couple of years ago after I received a death threat or two.'' That was pretty much the way it had gone down. When he'd started in the bounty hunting business he hadn't seen the need for a gun. He knew how to handle himself. But then he'd started tracking down the scum of the earth. It paid a hell of a lot better, but the risk was considerably greater. That's when he'd strapped on a weapon. He'd been carrying ever since.

She hugged her knees to her chest. ''How could this happen? You see these kinds of horrors in the movies, but you never think they'll happen to you.'' Her gaze connected with his once more. ''Will this ever be over?''

He didn't want to promise her anything he couldn't deliver. But he needed her to continue trusting him at least as much as she had so far. ''As long as you're not guilty of any wrongdoing, you're safe. It'll take some doing to square this but it can be done.''

''But I won't be safe unless they find the killer and we don't even have a clue as to his identity.''

''Unfortunately that's true. But we should focus on one step at a time.''

''What is the next step?''

''How about we make that decision in the morning?'' He gave her his most reassuring smile. ''We'll be able to think a lot more clearly then.''

She nodded. ''You're right.'' A new frown marred her brow. ''You're freezing.'' She touched his chest and another tremor went through him.

''I like the fresh air.'' He pushed up from the bed, knowing the continued contact would only lead to trouble. ''Good night.''

''G'night.'' She lay back on her pillows and snuggled under the covers.

He picked up his weapon. He didn't usually wander around without it. Just another indication of how far out of control his emotions were running. He switched off the table lamp and climbed onto the other bed, tucking the weapon under the pillow next to him. A few hours' shut-eye wouldn't hurt him, either. He was a light enough sleeper that any moves she made would wake him. He'd trained himself to be alert to his environment.

If she got any ideas about taking off, she wouldn't get far.

KELLY LAY perfectly still for so long that she almost fell asleep, but she forced her eyes to remain open. She waited and listened for Trent's breathing to grow slow and deep. A plan had been forming in her mind.

Well, at least, after she'd banished the very nearly overwhelming need to crawl into that bed with him. The sound of his breathing. Just knowing he was lying there had driven her crazy with need. She'd had to fight her traitorous body for long minutes to force her thoughts to the trouble she was in rather than the trouble she'd like to get into.

The disk, she reminded herself once more. She'd forwarded a copy of those files on the disk to her inbox just in case she lost the disk. The numbers were the key, she had decided. She had to try that possibility. If the answer to who had killed Ray and Ann lay in those files, she needed to know. She wanted her life back. The police knew she was still alive.

They hadn't mentioned Ann, but they were looking for Kelly Pruitt—for her. They hadn't offered a reward in connection with her but they had asked anyone who saw her to call in. She had to do something now. The killer would realize his mistake the moment he saw the news reports—if he hadn't already, considering the attack on them at Ann's house. Of course that move might be related to their cleaning up behind themselves as they had by burning the office.

Whatever they were up to, she had to act now.

Her gaze shifted to the other bed once more. He wanted to protect her…wanted to help her. She didn't doubt his sincerity. But she had to see for herself first…to be sure exactly what was on that disk before she included him. She had no reasonable motivation for her decision to keep him in the dark at this point. She just needed to do this. Ann and Ray were depending on her. Her whole life depended on that disk.

A full fifteen minutes after his respiration quieted to the point that she felt certain he'd fallen asleep, Kelly eased out of the bed. She padded noiselessly to the table where he'd left the room key next to his jacket. For about ten seconds she listened to ensure the rhythm of his breathing hadn't changed, then she slipped on her shoes and headed to the door.

She held her breath as she removed the chain and pulled back the dead bolt. A resounding *click* echoed through the room and her heart squeezed in her chest. Again she listened to his breathing pattern before making another move. Satisfied that he still slept, she eased the door open, praying it wouldn't squeak. She couldn't remember if it did or not.

Once she was outside she contemplated how she could camouflage herself so that the desk clerk didn't recognize her. She couldn't be sure how many times her face had run on the news today. By morning she'd be in all the papers. She wouldn't be safe anywhere.

She looked inside every car she passed in the parking lot until she found one that wasn't locked and contained something useful. Opening the door carefully, she slipped into the front passenger seat. She picked up the eyeglasses lying on the console and tried them on. The prescription blurred her vision but she could manage. Now, she needed something for her hair. She'd left her scarf and pins on the bedside table in the room.

In the glove box she found a wad of receipts with a rubber band around it. That would work. She tugged the rubber band free and tucked her hair back into a high ponytail. She surveyed her reflection and decided she looked different enough. In the picture they'd shown on television her hair had been down and, of course, she hadn't been wearing glasses.

Surveying the parking lot first, as she'd seen Trent do, she climbed out of the car, quietly closing the door behind her. She walked a bit unsteadily at first. The glasses, she realized. The prescription was so strong it made her dizzy. She'd have to remember to put the glasses back when she was finished. If the owner were driving she'd be down right dangerous without them.

Smoothing a hand over her clothes she almost laughed out loud at the thought that this clothing designer would be thrilled to hear that the outfit had held up extraordinary well in shoot-outs and rooftop escapes, oh, and plunges through the bushes.

Grabbing back her composure, she reminded herself that she couldn't let the hysteria claim her again. She had to be strong now. Had to focus.

In the lobby she produced a flirtatious smile for the young male clerk. "Hi," she said sweetly. "I can't sleep and I was wondering if there was some place around here I could check my e-mail." Some hotels provided such a service but she doubted this motel did. Still, it couldn't hurt to ask.

He dragged himself from his chair and used the counter to prop his chin on his hand. "Sorry we don't have a computer café or anything." He looked her up and down, openly drooling. "We do have complimentary coffee." He nodded to the table in the lobby that stank of coffee that had brewed far too long.

She sighed. "Darn. I was really hoping to get a little research done."

His forehead scrunched into a frown. "What kind of research?"

She smiled widely, plan B coming to her in a flash. "I'm a writer. I'm researching my next book." Well, Trent was a writer and he'd likely use this case in his novel. She was only using the truth to her advantage.

"Really? Wow." He looked her up and down again with a new kind of respect. "That's cool. What kind of book?"

"A murder mystery," she said, wagging her brows suggestively.

"Whoa." He glanced around the lobby. "I tell ya what, seeing that you're a writer and all, I could let you use the computer in my boss's office." He grinned. "Just don't tell anyone."

"That would be great." She glanced at his name-tag. "I could use a character named Tim. Would you mind?"

He blushed. "Cool." He gestured to the door behind him. "Come on, I'll show you the way."

Kelly waited for him as he exited the front desk area. "I really appreciate this," she said again.

Tim led her down a corridor marked Administration and to the second door on the right. "No sweat." He opened the door and flipped on the light. "Knock yourself out." He hesitated. "What was your name again?"

"Ann Romans," she said, coming up with the first name she could think of considering a bible verse from Romans was framed and hanging over his boss's desk.

"Let me know if you need anything else, Ann."

When he'd headed back to his station, Kelly settled behind the desk, pushed the glasses up on her head, and moved the mouse to shut down the screen saver. In mere seconds she was online. A few keystrokes later and she was reviewing the contents of her inbox. She clicked on the message that contained the files as an attachment and set to work trying to crack the password using variations of the numbers from Ray's office.

Dammit.

Nothing she did worked. She tried several more options and still came up dry. Massaging her forehead for a bit she considered all she knew about Ray's filing methods. How would he protect what he considered evidence?

A smile slid across her face. Of course. She typed in the word *evidence,* she did it over and over, each time typing in a different single digit until she got lucky.

Evidence7

The file opened and a list of seven sets of digits, each four in length, followed by another single set consisting of only three digits.

What was this? More coded files? She clicked on the first set of numbers but the file wouldn't open. She swore then clicked on the next one. Over and over she repeated the process to no avail.

Then she thought about the client numbers in Ray's Rolodex. What if each of these went with a name? Again, she tried name after name, but nothing happened.

She glanced at the clock and realized she'd been gone nearly half an hour. If Trent woke up she'd be in big trouble. She didn't need to push her luck where the guy running the desk was concerned, either. If he saw her face on the news recognition might just kick in.

Before she logged off the Net she decided to check Ann's files again. Now that she had some idea what was on the disk maybe something would click. Ann did have direct access to some of Ray's files. There might be something there she hadn't noticed before.

Kelly ran through the files one by one and came up empty-handed. There had to be some kind of connection that she was overlooking. She blew out a breath of frustration. She was too damned tired to think. Maybe Trent was right. She needed sleep. Tomorrow they would figure out the next step.

When she would have logged off she noticed the little icon indicating Ann had new mail in her inbox. That was odd. She hadn't received a single message in days.

Curious, Kelly opened the inbox and clicked on the waiting message.

Juliet, I've missed you terribly. Where have you been?

Romeo

Ice slid through Kelly's veins. This couldn't be. How could Ann get a message from Romeo if...

"Log off."

Startled, her gaze jerked upward to find Trent towering over her. "Log off," he repeated.

Her fingers trembling, she did as he commanded.

"Don't make a scene," he ordered in that same lethal tone. "Just come with me quietly and everything will be fine." He braced his right hand on his waist, pushing his jacket open in the process and allowing her to see the weapon strapped to his shoulder. "Now, *Kelly*."

He knew who she was.

A new wave of fear went through her.

But she had only one choice at the moment.

She did as he told her.

IT WAS PAST MIDNIGHT when the other car eased to a stop in front of his. Mac sat up a little straighter, annoyed that he'd been called out at this time of night to have to sit and wait for more than twenty minutes.

He watched the cartel's clean-up man emerge from his car and then saunter toward the passenger side of his. No matter that Mac knew they were both on the same team he couldn't help feeling uncomfortable in the man's presence. He was a stone-cold killer, ruthless. There was no telling how many men, and women, he'd killed in his career.

He got in and closed the door without saying a word.

"You got the word that Jarvis's office has been taken care of?" Mac asked. Hell somebody had to get this conversation started. He didn't plan to be here all frigging night. He had a life. This extracurricular work was getting in the way of everything lately. Hell, it wasn't his fault this jerk had screwed up.

"But they failed to get the Pruitt woman at Ann's condo." His voice was cold and carefully modulated. Anyone who heard it would likely recognize the underlying threat. Mac sure as hell did. His fingers itched to reach for his weapon but that would be fatal.

"No, they didn't get her. That P.I. helped her escape. His name is—"

"I know who he is," he cut Mac off. "What I don't know is why your people didn't spot the error days ago?" The subtle change in his careful tone made Mac even uneasier.

"I wasn't in charge of the investigation," he said flatly. "None of this would have happened if I'd been in charge." The whole frigging world was so focused on Jarvis and the federal agent who'd died that no one worried about the assistant. Until now.

Beady eyes filled with ice cut right through Mac even in the near darkness. "You have something to say, Agent McCade?"

Mac swallowed. "This was your hit man. He's the one who screwed up and killed the wrong woman. He made the mistake."

"No, McCade," he countered, "this fiasco was entirely my mistake."

Startled that he would admit the error, Mac waited for him to continue.

"I'd been watching Ann for two months. Playing a kind of game with her, Romeo to her Juliet. No matter how closely I looked I found nothing. She was trustworthy. Whatever went wrong with Jarvis had nothing to do with her. My only failure was in underestimating her attachment to the Pruitt woman. She disobeyed the cartel's direct order to stay clear of Jarvis and his assistant once the hit was ordered."

Mac frowned. "How do you figure that?"

"The man I contracted for the job swears there was no other woman in the office, that Ann was standing behind the desk as if she worked there. He, of course, thought she was Kelly Pruitt.

"I believe that Ann took the woman's place to prevent her death. She knew the hit had been ordered. There is no other explanation. The only question now is what does the Pruitt woman know?"

"I don't think she knows anything," Mac put in quickly. "Otherwise why would she run? Why not go to the police? I've had some of my friends watching for just that sort of move.''

"Who hired the P.I.?"

"Senator Lester," Mac said loathingly. "I don't know why that old bastard had to get involved."

"He has his reasons," the other man asserted. "There's a reason for everything."

"So why did you need to see me?" Mac asked, cutting to the chase. He didn't like being alone with this guy one little bit. "Is your shooter going to take care of his screwup and finish off Pruitt?"

The man smiled, it was sinister as hell and damned scary. "I have no tolerance for mistakes, McCade. He's dead, as you will be if you aren't careful."

"Nobody's more careful than me," Mac insisted, his heart fluttering at the implication. "I'm dedicated to duty. I won't let this investigation touch the cartel. You can be sure of that."

"I'm confident you won't," he said, his tone clearly amused.

"Who's going to take care of the woman and her P.I.?" Mac needed to know. Damn, he hoped like hell he wasn't going to have to do it. He wouldn't mind putting a bullet in the Pruitt woman's head, but he had no desire to tangle with the P.I.

"I'll be taking care of that personally," Mr. Clean said. "I won't risk failure by trusting anyone else. This one was too close." He shifted his gaze to Mac's. "Far too close."

Mac nodded. "I know what you mean."

"I may need your assistance," he continued, "can I count on you when the time comes?"

"Definitely," Mac assured him. "Is there any way I can help you locate her?" He'd been thinking about that. The senator would know where his hired help was. Mac could probably finagle that information from the old goat.

The other man shook his head. "I already know where they are."

Surprise slid through Mac. "That's good. Do you plan to interrogate her?" A thrill buzzed inside Mac at the prospect. He wouldn't mind doing a little poking and prodding with that pretty young thing himself.

"I don't intend to interrogate anyone," he said icily. "I'm going to kill them both."

Chapter Eleven

Trent stayed right behind Kelly as they exited the lobby via a side door so as not to attract the motel clerk's attention. Ire roared through him. Did she have no idea the kind of risk she'd taken? What if the clerk had recognized her and called the police? And opening that e-mail from Romeo... Hell, even going online to look at Ann Jones's files was dangerous. Why didn't she just put out an ad telling the world where she'd holed up for the night?

Did she really think she could break Jarvis's code?

Trent shook his head. It was time they got a few things straight. He should have been up front with her from the beginning. He sighed. But then she would have run again.

She stopped suddenly and jerked open a car door. Before he could question her action, she ripped the borrowed eyewear from her face and tossed them inside. He didn't miss the tremble in her hands as she jerked the rubber band from her hair and tossed it into the car as well. How could anyone consider her anything but innocent? She couldn't even steal a pair of glasses. That did little to relieve his irritation at the moment though. However afraid she was it did nothing to reduce the intensity of the furious glare she pointed in his direction. She slammed the car door and stormed the remaining distance to the room without a word, which he considered a blessing.

The last thing he wanted was to get into a shouting match with her at this hour of the morning. They definitely didn't need the attention.

She unlocked the door and went inside. He took a final look around the parking lot, then locked the door behind him.

"Get your things together, we're leaving," he ordered not bothering with an explanation. She could just figure it out since she thought she was so smart.

She whirled on him, rage sparkling in those hazel eyes. "I'm not going anywhere with you." She pointed a finger at him. "I don't even know who you are."

"At least I didn't lie about my name," he tossed back as he gathered his duffel bag and surveyed the room for anything he might have overlooked.

Her fury faltered ever so slightly. "I…I didn't know for sure if I could trust you."

He gritted his teeth until he'd subdued his own swiftly building rage. He couldn't decide who he was madder at, her or himself. She'd slipped out of the room while he slept! Not once since he'd started tracking knuckleheads stupid enough to skip out on their bail had he let down his guard so completely. She could have gotten into real trouble—while he slept! Sleep deprivation was no excuse.

"Maybe you should have thought of that when you were coming on to me." Whether she'd trusted him or not, she'd sure as hell wanted to jump into bed with him. Somehow that disappointed him. He wanted what she felt for him to be about more than mere sex.

That final realization startled him. What the hell was he thinking? Sex was good. Hell, sex was great.

But this was an assignment...it wasn't personal.

He shook himself and focused on the matter at hand: getting out of here before the guys who wanted her dead showed up. If they were monitoring her Internet account or Ann's, as he suspected, in an attempt to track her whereabouts, they were likely on their way already.

Her mouth gaped at his remark. If she'd looked furious a few moments ago, she looked downright ready to go off now. "You were the one who kissed me!"

Like he could forget that. Heat scorched through him all over again at even the thought of how it had felt to kiss her.

"We don't have time for this," he urged. "We have to get out of here." He didn't bother to remind her that she'd invited him to bed.

She shook her head with far too much enthusiasm. "No way am I going anywhere with you until you tell me exactly who you are and why you pretended to be Romeo."

Dammit, didn't she get it? They had to leave *now*. "I'm a private investigator hired by Senator Lester to find out who ordered a hit on Raymond Jarvis," he said in a rush. "I figured out you were alive the day I arrived in Texas and decided you were either one of the bad guys or a victim on the run. The Romeo thing was the only lead I could find in a hurry that would give me an inside track with you." He gentled his voice, let her see his frustration. "I'm trying to help you."

For three long beats he wasn't sure if he'd swayed her or not, but then her expression softened. "Why are we leaving?" she asked, the fervor gone from her tone, leaving a weariness that he could sympathize with.

"They may have a tracer on Ann's inbox. They could be on their way here right now. We can't take that risk." He shrugged. "Not to mention that the motel clerk has seen you. It's not safe to stay in either case."

She reached for her jacket and purse. "All right." She looked around the room as if searching for something she'd forgotten. When her gaze bumped into his once more, she looked contrite. "I'm sorry I lied to you. I was scared."

One side of his mouth hitched into a smile in an attempt to lessen the tension. "Let's call it even."

Kelly felt tremendously relieved as they loaded into Trent's truck and headed for the highway. She hadn't liked lying to him. She was glad the truth was out in the open now. Stealing a glance at him, she shivered at the memory of that kiss. He was right, she had come on to him. More than once.

Maybe it was the stress. She certainly didn't usually behave this way.

She faced forward and forced thoughts of his body and how incredible sex would likely be with him from her mind.

That act of futility lasted about five seconds.

His presence was entirely overwhelming. She couldn't *not* think about him. His scent, clean soap and hot, hard male, drove her crazy. The tension vibrating from that amazing frame made her want to squirm. No way could she ignore him in this cramped cab.

He swore beneath his breath. She winced. Had he read her mind again? The guy had to be psychic.

"We've got a tail."

"What?" She whipped around to peer out the back window.

"Hold on," he warned.

The warning he'd issued didn't penetrate quickly enough. The truck swerved hard to the right and she experienced an up-close encounter with the passenger side window.

Tires squealed and the engine roared as he slammed his foot down on the accelerator. The truck rocketed forward, propelling her back against the seat. Her pounding heart blasted into her throat, cutting off her ability to breathe as she latched onto the armrest for an anchor.

Despite his evasive maneuvers those headlights came into view behind them once more. Kelly gripped the armrest with all her might and prayed hard and fast that Trent could outwit their pursuers. He whipped to the left and she rode out the force of inertia. Right again before lunging forward.

A loud crack to her right jerked her attention in that direction. A good portion of the side mirror was now missing. Her heart dropped all the way to her stomach and quivered helplessly. Fear gripped her throat.

"Get down!" he bellowed.

He didn't have to tell her twice. Shoving aside the shoulder restraint, she hunkered down in the seat as far as the lap belt would allow. She could feel the truck swerving, swaying, charging forward. More pings and cracks told her that weapons were being fired at them.

She should do something. Use his gun and fire back. She'd never fired a weapon before but she could figure it out. When she lifted her head to suggest just that, he shouted, "Stay down!"

Cowering in the seat, she closed her eyes and prayed some more. She didn't want to die like this…a fugitive, possibly suspected of murder. And she damn sure didn't want to leave this earth without being kissed by Trent Tucker again.

He made a hard right, slammed on the brakes.

She jerked upright, the sudden stop of the vehicle forcing her forward. It was too dark to see anything. She looked around…tried to assimilate what she saw. An alley between two buildings.

"Run!"

He was out of the truck, duffel in hand, before the word fully registered in her brain. She bolted out the door and hurried toward where he waited at the front of the vehicle. He grabbed her hand and raced forward, into the darkness.

By the time they reached the end of the alley she heard the squeal of brakes and tires behind them...back where they'd left the truck.

"Keep moving," he growled, dragging her forward when her feet slowed.

The crack of a shot hit something a few feet away. The brick wall of the building on her right. They were aiming for her first.

She ran harder, forcing her much shorter legs to keep up with his long strides. She would not let that bastard kill her. He'd killed her best friend and her boss. He wasn't going to get away with it. To ensure that he didn't she had to stay alive. She didn't know his face, but she did know his voice.

At the point where the buildings backed up to the ones on the next block he took a left, then a right between two adjacent warehouses. Vaguely she recognized the area as the warehouse district. No one would be around at this time of night. Most of the warehouses had been renovated into businesses. There was a jail...she couldn't remember the address. Cops would be there...

Trent just kept running, pulling her this way and that, weaving between buildings. Her lungs burned for air. Her legs felt rubbery, but she kept on running.

He dragged her into a dark building...a garage.

Ducking between two parked vehicles he dragged her down to the floor.

"Stay here. Don't come out for any reason. I'll be back for you."

She wanted to tell him to be careful...to hold on

to him for a second longer, but he was gone before she could react or catch her breath enough to speak.

She sat there for a long while, her breath charging in and out of her lungs. Her whole body quivered with exhaustion.

As she plummeted from the rush of adrenaline she became more aware of her surroundings. Dark. The place smelled of grease and gasoline. She looked toward the aisle that separated the rows where cars parked. Why were there cars in here at this time of the morning? Some manufacturing company that worked around the clock, she supposed. A shipping business, maybe.

Feeling exposed she crawled toward the wall and the front of the cars. She eased between the wall and the nose of one of the vehicles and hugged her arms around her.

The quiet pressed down on her and she struggled with the trembling rampant in her body. Where was Trent? How long had he been gone? It felt like forever but was probably only a few minutes. He'd said he would be back for her. Was he trying to stop the guy or just lead him away from her? She didn't like either scenario.

The tiniest rasp of sound reached her ears. She froze. Listened. The urge to run raced through her. She had to be still…be perfectly quiet. Couldn't even breathe.

The whisper of fabric against metal.

Closer.

She squinted into the darkness, tried to see anything.

Movement near the driver's side door of the car shielding her from view.

She braced herself for discovery…balled her fists to fend off her attacker.

"It's me."

Trent.

A ragged breath escaped her trembling lips.

"You scared the hell out of me."

He dropped down onto the concrete floor next to her. "I lost him, but we're staying put until dawn just in case."

She nodded, too weak with relief to manage a response. The cold seemed to leech into her very bones. She shivered and hugged herself more tightly. God, she was so cold.

"It's okay." His strong arms went around her and pulled her close to that powerful chest. "We're okay," he murmured.

She snuggled against him, needing his warmth and she knew with certainty that, for now, they were okay. She had her cowboy protector.

As soon as it was light, Trent and Kelly went out onto the street again. Rather than going back to the truck, he opted to lay low in a diner until regular business hours. Using a credit card and driver's license with an alias he carried for just such an occasion, he rented a car and drove to a ritzy hotel downtown. He sprung for a bridal suite and let the clerk know that he didn't want to be disturbed. Grinning knowingly she assured him that he needn't worry.

He'd left Kelly in the room and gone shopping.

They both needed a change of clothes and a little cash would be useful. The purchases for himself were a breeze, but hers were a little more complicated. Knowing she couldn't afford to be seen in public any more than absolutely necessary, she'd given him her sizes.

The jeans and blouse and footwear hadn't been a problem. But the undergarments were proving more of a challenge. Should he go with plain and functional or lacy and sexy? He remembered well her personal preference. He'd gotten a good look when he'd checked out her town house. Just touching the feminine lingerie had him imagining her wearing those and nothing else. A vivid mental picture of her, clad in the naughty black silk, sitting astride that saddle in her bedroom gave him an immediate hard-on.

Grabbing a handful of lace and silk, including a nightgown, he paid for the purchases and got the hell out of the lust-inspiring boutique. Before going back to the hotel he stopped by a drugstore and picked up the necessary toiletries for an extended stay.

He entered the room, instantly going on alert.

Where the hell was she?

His gaze landed on a room service cart and a frown worked its way across his forehead. An empty ice bucket and a single champagne flute stood on the cart.

Gently scented steam hit his nostrils, drawing his gaze to the half-open bathroom door. He dropped the packages on the massive bed and strode cautiously toward the bathroom. When he peeked inside his entire body spasmed with need.

Neck deep in bubbles, she lounged in the whirlpool

tub made for two. A half-empty champagne bottle sat on the marble ledge. The twin to the champagne flute he'd seen on the cart was held delicately between her fingers. She sipped the champagne, then set it aside and reached for another succulent strawberry dipped in chocolate.

He started to ask her what the hell she was doing, but he didn't want to break the spell. Simply watching her enthralled him, stiffened muscles already hard with need. He allowed the fantasy for a few minutes longer, but guilt forced him to make his presence known.

"I'm back," he announced.

She gasped, the golden bubbly in the glass halfway to that luscious mouth. "You scared the heck out of me again."

Her voice sounded a little thick…a little syrupy slow.

"What're you doing?" He nodded to the bottle.

"Getting drunk," she said flatly. "What does it look like?"

"You think that's a good idea?" He moved across the room and picked up the bottle.

She stared up at him petulantly. "Frankly, I don't care if it's a good idea." Her expression turned brazen then. "Since you won't distract me with mind-boggling sex, I might as well distract myself." She reached for another strawberry, inadvertently—or maybe not—revealing the sweet curve of one breast.

"I'll…ah…" He swallowed hard, his throat abruptly dry. "I'll bring your stuff in here."

Turning his back on the sensual picture of her in

that tub, naked save for those bubbles, he strode back into the room and deposited the remainder of the champagne on the cart. He gathered the bags containing the items he'd bought for her and took them to the bathroom. He left them on the floor, careful not to look her way and exited, closing the door behind him.

She muttered something that sounded a lot like *jerk* but he only smiled. He wasn't immune to her by any means, but he knew she would regret the move in the end. He wished he could be the hero and claim he was protecting her virtue, but that would be a lie. He just couldn't bear the thought of her regretting anything between them. As much as he wanted her, he could wait until their coming together was on a level playing field with no outside interference.

Trent wasn't sure when he'd decided that his feelings went that deep and he was probably a fool, but that's just the way it was. Right now, he had to focus on stopping the man determined to kill her.

KELLY WOKE UP face-down on the bed. The back of her head throbbed as if she'd been bludgeoned with a blunt object. She groaned and attempted to roll over.

Too much.

She dropped her face back into the pillow.

''Champagne hangover's the worst,'' a distinctly male voice said from the other side of the bed.

She jerked her head up and winced at the scream of protest from deep inside her skull. When she could open her eyes again she glared at the handsome face smiling down at her. Trent, pillows propped behind him on the headboard, reclined leisurely on the other side of the bed.

Three feet of satin sheets spanned the meager distance between them. The ache in her head was suddenly overridden by an insistent pulse between her thighs.

"What time is it?" She licked her lips and tasted toothpaste. She vaguely remembered climbing out of the tub and brushing her teeth. Another memory zinged her...lacy, silky panties and bras. How had he known what she liked?

Her eyes rounded and her mouth yawned open as she recalled tugging on a pair of the sexy undies and the matching bra then prancing into the bedroom just to tease him.

Only to pass out.

But not before she saw the gleam of male approval in those blue eyes.

He'd covered her. Her fingers fisted in the sheet. Thank God.

"Seven-thirty," he said in answer to her question.

Heavens, she'd slept the entire afternoon. The hangover intruded once more and she groaned, wishing he'd simply shoot her and get her out of her misery.

"There's aspirin and water on the table beside you," he said quietly, kindly keeping his voice low in deference to her aching head.

She eased up onto one elbow and downed a couple of aspirins, along with a full glass of water. The urge to pee hit her with extreme urgency. Her breath caught. Did she ignore it and hope it passed or did she admit defeat and give him a good look at her all but naked again?

"There's a gown at your feet."

There he went reading her mind again. Too humiliated to analyze the recurring phenomenon, she reached for the gown, jerked it over her head and dashed into the bathroom.

When she'd relieved herself, she washed her hands and stared at her mussed reflection. Her face was flushed and her hair was tousled. She looked a fright. But the skimpy jade gown looked good on her. She stared down at herself. Did he find her attractive? Is that why he'd picked this gown?

Kelly rolled her eyes and decided to brush her teeth again. She'd lost it, that was all she could say on her behalf. All it had taken was a few hours trapped with a handsome cowboy and she'd turned into a slut.

TRENT'S CELL PHONE rang and he snatched it up. It was about time. He'd been expecting to hear from Heath for hours now. "Tucker."

"We broke the code—at least part of it." He'd known that Trent was waiting for word from him so he hadn't bothered with perfunctory greetings. "The file lists seven accounts that Jarvis apparently considered suspect. With each account there's detailed chronology of activity. The money is moved back and forth between the accounts like a chess game. All seven accounts are owned by Renaissance."

"Any luck on tracking down shareholders?"

"I believe the last file contains that information. We haven't been able to open it yet. It's encoded a little differently. The guy at N.S.A. is working on it. We're getting closer on the girlfriend. I may have an address for you later tonight.''

Both of which meant more time. Considering the ease with which their hit man located them, he was one smart guy. But Trent was no dummy himself. He could evade the bastard a little while longer.

''Any word from Detective Hargrove?'' Trent didn't like that he'd been kept out of the picture so long. That part didn't sit right with him. A simple debrief didn't take that long.

''The feds are still holding him according to Senator Lester.'' Heath hesitated. ''That's mainly why I'm calling. The senator has contacted me twice in the past hour. He insisted that I call you and set up this meet.''

''What kind of meet?'' Trent wasn't ready to let anyone else other than Heath know his location.

''Special Agent McCade from the Houston Bureau office wants a face-to-face. He says he has information pertinent to the case. The senator doesn't know for sure if he's on the up and up, but he believes the man may be prepared to offer additional info from the Bureau.''

From the Houston office, not the Dallas office where the dead agent had been assigned. ''It's worth looking into,'' Trent agreed. ''He may know what Agent Davis was up to.''

''Then again,'' Heath countered, ''it could be a setup by the feds to lure you and Ms. Pruitt in. They're getting pretty restless. They've contacted Ian already wanting to know your whereabouts. They've even threatened legal action if he doesn't provide your location.''

That could get sticky. "See if you can get the senator to get the feds off our backs and I'll see what McCade has to say. Where does he want to meet?''

Heath gave him the address of an uptown supper club. "He said he'd be there at nine.''

Trent glanced at his watch. Almost 8:00 p.m. "Tell him I'll be there, but if anything looks fishy I'm walking away.''

"Where are we going?'' Kelly asked as he put away his phone.

One look at her standing there in that jade gown obliterated all other thought. God she was beautiful.

"You're not going anywhere without me, Trent Tucker, so don't play dumb.''

Dumb was not nearly a strong enough adjective to describe his inability to pull it together and the next thirty minutes proved the point.

Kelly couldn't believe she'd had to argue with him for more than a half hour to convince him that she should come along. Whatever this FBI agent had to say, she had a right to hear it. She glared at Trent's stony profile. Just because he had the gun didn't mean he was the boss.

She looked away just as quickly. Though he did possess other assets that could sway her given the proper timing, this was not the time.

He drove through Houston's Richmond Entertainment District passing a string of themed bars and elegant restaurants until he arrived at the Longhorn

Supper Club. She doubted either of them was dressed suitably, but that wasn't going to stop them.

When he'd surveyed the front of the club and the parking area, he drove down the block, choosing to park at a jam-packed sports bar. He tucked the car keys under the floor mat and turned his attention to her.

"If anything goes wrong in there I want you to run like hell, get in this car…" He placed his cell phone in the glove box. "Press redial on my cell and tell Heath Murphy to get you out of Texas."

She huffed at his suggestion. "And where will you be?"

"I'll be providing the distraction that gives you the opportunity to run since you were too hardheaded to stay at the hotel."

Her pulse leaped at the idea that he might be hurt if there was trouble. Maybe she should have stayed at the hotel. No. That wouldn't have protected him.

"That discussion is over. Let's not waste any more time."

They emerged from the car and Trent led the way down an alley so that they could approach the Longhorn via the back. Nothing looked out of place in the vicinity of the club. But there was no way to be certain.

Trent hesitated at the door. "Stay behind me and get the hell out of here at the first sign of trouble."

She grabbed him by the arm. "Wait." When he turned to face her she went up on tiptoe and dragged his mouth down to hers. She kissed him with all the fear and need churning inside her. If she was going to get killed tonight, she wanted to die with the taste of his lips on hers.

When she drew back he stared into her eyes for one endless moment before turning back to the door.

Her hands shook when she swiped her palms on her slacks. She did not want to die tonight. And she damned sure didn't want him to. But, as this point, they had no guarantees of tomorrow.

The hostess met them in the vestibule. "Good evening, do you have a reservation?"

"I believe another member of our party is already here," Trent told her. "McCade is the name."

The hostess glanced at her clipboard. "Yes. They arrived about ten minutes ago."

They?

Trent exchanged a look with Kelly. This was bad. He didn't have to say anything. She knew.

He and Kelly followed the hostess through the dimly lit club, weaving around one occupied table or booth after the other. A band played on the stage on one side of the large room, a dance floor directly in front of them. The music wasn't overwhelmingly loud, but between it and the buzz of dozens of conversations it was definitely hard to hear. None of which helped her lingering headache. *Note to self,* she chided, *never drink champagne again.*

As they neared the far side of the dining room, Trent pulled Kelly close to his side. "Don't forget what I said. Call Heath. He'll help you."

Her heart floundered in her chest, its frantic flailing doing nothing to help her catch her breath.

"Right over there, sir," the hostess said as she gestured to the booth in the far corner. "Your waitress will be right with you."

Trent led the way to the booth. Kelly blinked as they neared it. There was only one person occupying the booth, his back turned to their approach. Hadn't the hostess said "They"?

As she and Trent came around to the side of the booth Agent McCade's head lolled to one side. Kelly frowned. What...her gaze focused on the center of his chest where a small hole marred his shirt. Massive amounts of blood had leaked from the seemingly innocuous little hole, turning his pale gray shirt a sinister crimson.

Like Ann's blouse.

And just like Ann, McCade was dead.

Chapter Twelve

"We have to get out of here," Trent said tautly.

Kelly didn't move. She just stood there staring at the dead agent.

"Ya'll ready to order your drinks?"

The waitress.

A scream rent the air.

In mere seconds the entire restaurant was in utter chaos.

Trent ushered Kelly toward the door marked Employees Only. They burst through the kitchen amid a roar of protests and ran for the back door.

"He's dead!" Kelly shouted at Trent as he dragged her down the alley.

"We will be too if we don't get out of here."

His weapon palmed, he didn't let up, forcing her to keep up with his pace.

As they moved from one parking lot to another a shot whizzed right between them, scarcely missing her.

"Dammit," he muttered. "Stay down."

They crouched as low as they could and moved

from car to car. Trent returned fire, unable to slow down long enough to do anything more than get a general location on the guy.

Almost there.

He could see his rental car on the other side of the sports bar lot. Kelly huddled next to him. They were more or less trapped, but the sound of sirens in the distance would provide some relief.

"When I give you the word, run like hell. Get the car started and head toward the street. I'll catch up to you."

"Why can't you go with me?"

Another shot pinged metal a few feet away.

"Go!"

She hesitated only a second, then she ran. He laid down a rapid pattern of ground fire to distract the shooter. When he heard the rental car's engine start, he started to move. He had to get this guy moving in the other direction, then double back and catch up with her.

Kelly jammed the gearshift into drive and stamped on the gas pedal. Her palms were sweating so she clenched the steering wheel tighter. Stay calm... focus.

She circled a row of cars and barreled toward the street.

Where was he?

The strobe of blue lights momentarily distracted her as a profusion of police cruisers descended upon the parking lot at the Longhorn.

She heard another gunshot. Whipped her head in that direction at the same instant she slammed on her brakes before charging onto the street. Horns blared as the nose of her car nudged into the oncoming traffic.

Something hard hit the passenger side of the car. She jumped, looked up in time to see Trent jerk the door open and dive in. "Go!" he shouted.

She plunged into the traffic, earning herself more horn blasts of protest. She drove away from the blue lights...away from the threat though she knew he could be right behind her.

"Faster," Trent growled.

She floored the accelerator. "I'm doing the best I can."

"Drive until you're certain you've lost him. Don't stop for anything."

He sounded funny...breathless and...

He was bleeding. Her gaze riveted to the gash in his forehead.

A horn blared.

She jerked the wheel to force her car back into the right lane. "Trent!"

She kept one hand on the steering wheel and shook him with the other. "Trent! Talk to me, dammit!"

He was out...or dead.

Frantic now, she fumbled around on his neck feeling for a pulse. Relief shook her to the very core of her being when she felt the steady drumming.

"Thank God," she murmured. "Thank God."

Forcing her full attention to the street now, she gripped the steering wheel with both hands and drove the same way Trent had last night. Taking sudden turns, weaving through alleys. Anything to lose whoever might be following her. Now and again she checked his pulse, thankful each time that she found his heart still beating.

Should she go to a hospital?

Back to the hotel?

What did she do?

Gunshot wounds were reported to the police.

Could she risk the police being called?

Could she risk him dying?

She needed to stop and check out his injury.

Someplace safe.

Her thoughts stilled.

Her place.

She didn't live far from here. Who would ever look for her there? It was the last place on earth the police or anyone else would expect her to go.

Decision made, she drove even faster.

By the time she arrived at her place he was coming around. He groaned then opened his eyes.

"Do I need to take you to a hospital?" she demanded, fear making her voice too high.

"I'll be all right." He touched his bleeding forehead and winced. There was so much blood. "Where are we?"

"My place."

He looked surprised but didn't argue.

"Can you walk?" she asked.

"I think so."

She helped him out of the car, put an arm around his waist and supported as much of his weight as she could.

At her door, she propped him against the wall and

fumbled beneath a potted plant for her spare key. When she'd gotten the door open, she led him inside and then locked it once more.

She didn't bother turning on a light, she knew her way around. The bathroom had no exterior windows so turning on a light in there would be safe.

"Sit right here and I'll get my first aid kit," she instructed, gesturing to the toilet.

Not waiting for a response she rushed to the kitchen and dug beneath the sink until she found the first aid kit she'd bought when she first moved into the apartment.

In the bathroom Trent had already started to clean his wound. "It's not that bad," he told her. "Head wounds always bleed a lot," he reminded for her benefit.

"But you blacked out?"

"I took a fall when the bullet grazed me. I think maybe it stunned me."

She set the kit on the counter and braced herself against the doorframe. Her entire body trembled and her knees felt weak enough to give way under her. Tonight had been too close. And still they knew nothing about the killer.

How the hell did he know their every move?

When Trent had the bleeding under control she'd pulled herself together once more. She insisted on taking over from there. "Sit," she ordered.

He peeled off his bloody jacket and shirt and tossed them aside. She swallowed tightly, trying her level best not to be distracted by that bare chest.

He probably needed stitches, but telling him would

be pointless. She taped the cut together as best she could, liberally applying antibiotic cream, then covered the whole thing with gauze and more tape. He'd taken a knock on the head all right. He had a good-size lump, but his pupils were normal and responsive. She stepped back slightly and surveyed her handiwork. At least the bleeding had stopped.

She washed her hands and dampened a washcloth to clean up his face and neck. There was still blood here and there. He'd gotten the worst of it. Over and over she rinsed the cloth and rubbed at his bare skin, removing the final remnants of drying blood. By the time she'd finished her stomach was in knots.

"I'll make some tea," she said, needing space. Needing to concentrate on anything but his injured body. He could have been killed.

And it would have been her fault.

Before going to the kitchen she went upstairs to her room allowing the dark to conceal the emotions she didn't want to feel or reveal to anyone else. Tears were spilling down her cheeks by the time she closed herself up in her closet. She cried for a while…she didn't know how long.

How had this happened to her? She just wanted her life back…wanted to right the wrong that had been done to her friends.

She flung off her clothes…clothes stained with his blood. What if he'd been killed tonight? She'd already had one person she cared about die for her. She couldn't bear to lose anyone else…especially not Trent.

Groping in the dark she reached for her robe. She

wrapped it around her and inhaled the familiar and comforting scent of home.

She just wanted all this to go away.

A soft knock came at the door. "Kelly, are you okay?"

Was she okay?

Of course she wasn't okay.

"No," she said hoarsely.

What was he, dumb or something?

"Can I come in?"

She choked out a laugh. "Sure."

He opened the closet door and stepped inside. "Is there a light in here?"

"There's a switch by the door." She sniffed.

He fumbled on the wall until he located the switch then the overhead light came on. One of the fluorescent bulbs was dead so the glow the lone bulb offered wasn't anything to brag about. Kind of like her life, she realized. She was all alone, with nothing but heartache ahead of her.

If that hit man didn't kill her.

How pathetic was that?

"We're okay," Trent assured her.

"For how long?" she argued, glaring at him through the tears. "He'll just come after us again. We don't even know who he is. How can we stop a nameless, faceless threat?" She scrubbed at her eyes, furious with herself for crying.

He started to reach out to her then, apparently, thought better of it. Just her luck. "We'll figure this out. No matter how long it takes. I won't let anything

happen to you. I'll do everything in my power to protect you.''

She laughed and jammed her fingers through her
hair. "Don't you get it?" she demanded. "It's not me
I'm worried about!" She shoved at his chest, wanting
to push him away but failing miserably. He was too
strong…too big. "It's you I'm worried about, you big
dummy."

He reached for her. She fought him, tried to bat his
hands away, but he pulled her against him all the
same. Her efforts were useless against his strength.

He didn't say anything, just held her. What was
there to say anyway? She'd spoken her piece, made
a fool of herself. What did she expect? At least he
understood and didn't say something lame that would
make her feel even stupider.

When he finally drew back, he smiled down at her,
the beauty of that smile took her breath away, made
her knees go weak all over again. "What do you say
we sit for a while and talk. Maybe have that tea you
mentioned."

She nodded, too afraid to speak. If she opened her
mouth again she might just say something else totally
inane. But whose brain wouldn't go to mush under
the circumstances?

In her bedroom he paused. "You like cowboys,
huh?" He looked from the framed print to the saddle
her daddy had given her.

The light from the closet didn't afford much visi-
bility she knew the details of the picture as well
as the saddle by heart.

"My mother got the picture for me on my sixteenth

birthday." She smiled as the pleasant memories flooded back. "She said it was to remind me that the only good men were cowboys." She blushed, thinking how foolish she must sound. He hadn't asked for a biography. "And the saddle was a high school graduation gift from my dad. He died not long after that so I decided to have it mounted on a base so I could use it for a piece of furniture and look at it whenever I wanted to and remember him. Who needs a horse to admire a fine saddle?"

"Sounds like you had some great folks," he said softly. Trent could feel the tension in her. She was having trouble calming down after their latest brush with death. He was having a little trouble himself but it had nothing to do with the hit man he'd tangled with.

"They were the best," she agreed before clamping down on her trembling bottom lip.

"How about that tea?" he suggested with as much cheer as he could muster.

She looked up at him, that watery gaze connecting fully with his. "Distract me, Trent." She closed her eyes and shook her head. "I don't want to think anymore."

A jolt of need went through him. "Do you have any idea how much I'd like to do that?" He took her hand in his. "But I don't want you to regret it and I'm afraid, under the circumstances, you would."

She shook her head and in one smooth motion untied the sash to her robe and allowed it to fall to the floor. "The only regret I'll have," she said huskily, "is if I don't do this right now."

He tried to control the impulse but it was impossible. The sight of her in those lacy black panties and that barely there satin bra kicked all other thought from his skull. "You're beautiful," he murmured before licking his lips hungrily. He couldn't have been more obvious. He wanted her. Wanted her here and now. But he shouldn't.

In about the sexiest move he'd ever been privy to, she straddled that glossy leather saddle and looked him square in the eye. "Take your clothes off, cowboy." She pressed her thighs tightly on either side of that saddle horn and his whole body jerked with need. *"Now."*

There wasn't that much to take off and he was way past arguing with himself.

He tugged off first one boot and then the other, his gaze never leaving her. Her hands moved over her body, teasing him, making him sweat. He unbuttoned his fly and slowly lowered the zipper, his skin catching on fire as the realization penetrated that he was going to have her completely. When he shoved his jeans and briefs over his hips she started to rock, back and forth, on the saddle, her breath catching at the sensual sensation the movement elicited.

He shucked the jeans and briefs, kicked them aside. His body was already fully aroused and standing at attention. She looked at him and smiled, then licked her lips.

He swore softly. At this rate this thing was going to be over before they started. He went to her, slid his arms around her waist and lifted her against him, closing his mouth over hers before she could protest the move. He kissed her hard and long, thrust his tongue deep inside her sweet mouth the same way he wanted to plunge another part of his anatomy into her body.

He lowered her onto the bed, not breaking the contact of their lips. He swore again when his fingers encountered the satin encasing her breasts. He'd forgotten all about her flimsy attire. Jerking the bra down, he fastened his mouth over one breast. She cried out with pleasure. He lathed that breast, sucked and nibbled until his sex throbbed in warning. Resisting the urgency to get straight to the heart of the matter, he moved to the other breast, tugged on its taut nipple with his teeth. Her hands urged him on, tracing the corded muscles of his back and shoulders. He fumbled with the closure to her bra, not wanting to take his attention away from her sweet flesh. He pulled the confining garment away from her body, tossed it across the bed and burrowed his face between those ripe breasts.

He dragged the panties down her legs and followed the path with his mouth. He wanted to taste all of her…wanted to eat her up. Her breath came in ragged spurts, her slim rib cage rising and falling frantically. He pressed his mouth between her thighs, loving the salty essence of her. She screamed his name and damn if he didn't almost come against her skin. He refused to give in, he had to hear…had to feel her climax first. She deserved that at the very least.

Her fingers tangled in his hair as he delved more deeply with his tongue, searching for that certain spot that would drive her wild. She arched up to meet him.

And then her body shuddered and convulsed, a primal cry tearing from her lips. He held her, watched her come apart with release.

He couldn't wait any longer...had to be inside her. He kissed his way up her body, positioning himself for maximum thrust.

She moved.

Scrambled away from him.

She climbed off the bed and held out her hand to him, wriggling her fingers for him to join her. The flow of blood to his groin depleting his brain and disabling his ability to speak, he moved helplessly, mutely to join her.

She pulled him to where the saddle stood. "Sit," she ordered.

For one second Kelly was sure he would refuse. The haze of lust cleared fractionally and he looked from her to the saddle and back. But then he complied. Straddled it as if it had been made for him.

Her body still quivered with release, making her unsteady on her feet, but she couldn't wait to feel him inside her. She started to climb on with him but he stopped her.

"My wallet," he murmured thickly. "Condom."

She hadn't thought of that. He hadn't, either, apparently, until now. The building urgency propelling her, she fumbled in his back pocket for his wallet. Her fingers awkward with impatience, she finally dug the package free and handed it to him. He tore it open and sheathed it over his thick, upright sex. Fire roared through her veins, settling between her thighs. She couldn't wait any longer.

She straddled his lap facing him, standing on tiptoe so that he could position himself beneath her. She felt the nudge of his tip and moaned with delight.

"You're killing me," he groaned, his body taut, granite hard.

Smiling wickedly, she eased downward, encasing him one rock solid inch at a time. Her fingers dug into his shoulders as she started to pant, unable to control the pounding of her heart...by the time she'd sheathed him fully her body was on the verge of orgasm again. She closed her eyes and pressed down, making the seal complete. He made a sound... savage...primal. She cried out in answer. The incredible pressure of him filling her so completely had pleasure warring with pain...anticipation battling with hesitation. His own breath catching, he bracketed her hips with his hands and rocked her gently. The sensation exploded through her, making her entire body quiver deliciously. Again and again he rocked her that way...gently, sensually.

She braced her hands on his sweat-slickened chest, the feel of his heart pounding beneath her palms adding to her mushrooming excitement. The pull of release started way down deep inside, yanked at her patience. Made her squirm with restlessness. She wanted it...needed it...now! She whimpered in desperation. His body perfectly attuned to hers, he rocked her harder against him, pressed her hips down more fully onto his. Her body convulsed in reaction. She wanted to scream in ecstasy but his powerful moves, the way those intense blue eyes looked straight into hers, rendered her incapable of making a sound.

And then she flew over the edge once more, the sounds coming from her throat so savage they had to have been prompted by some ancient, primitive gene. He came too...the eruption affecting his entire body. That sculpted frame tensed to the point of snapping, his conquering groan every bit as primitive as her own, and then he relaxed, his breath raging in and out of him. The feel of him pulsing inside her as he wrapped his arms around her and pulled her against his chest made her want to weep with joy...with utter, blissful fulfillment.

Even if her life ended tomorrow...she would have this perfect moment.

Chapter Thirteen

Trent sat on the edge of the bed and watched Kelly sleep. He couldn't bear to wake her. It was still early, just past 7:00 a.m. The sheet draped the curves of her body making him want to crawl beneath those covers again and cuddle up next to her. Her silky blond hair splayed over the pink pillow, making his fingers itch to thread through it.

His gaze shifted to the saddle mounted on that thick pedestal. She'd definitely rocked his world on that baby. He couldn't imagine ever making love again without thinking of that moment…of her. He doubted he would ever do anything again without thoughts of her slipping into the equation.

He was done for.

She'd marked him…branded his heart with her touch and he was pretty sure there wasn't a vaccine for this malady.

He looked at the framed image hanging on her wall and recalled her mother's advice about cowboys. It had been a good long while since he'd played the part of cowboy. Getting in too deep had damaged him and he'd decided that being that kind of hero wasn't worth the price. He'd been too sure of himself, gotten personally involved in the lives of that woman and her son. And in the end he hadn't been able to save them. He'd promised himself then and there that he would never let his emotions rule him again.

He shook his head at his own weakness. And look what he'd done. This time it was even more disturbing. He was pretty sure this go-around that he was in love with the woman involved. Last time she'd only been a friend. He just wasn't sure he could be the kind of cowboy Kelly apparently wanted in her life.

But he could protect her until this was over.

Everything else could be worked out after that.

She was so young. He sighed as his gaze settled on that angelic face once more. More than ten years younger than him. Did they have anything in common other than mind-blowing sex? How in hell could he have let things go this far? He had no answer for that one. It simply was. Had been since the moment he laid eyes on her.

He'd showered and dressed, pulling on an oversize T-shirt from her closet to go with his jeans since his shirt was bloodstained. He didn't even mind the pink logo on the black T. It read: Girl Power. He was all for that.

He needed to call in, touch base with Heath. It dawned on him then that his cell phone was in the glove box of the rental car. Heath could have been trying to reach him.

Slipping quietly from the room, Trent made his way downstairs and outside. The air was cool and a soft mist was falling. The overcast sky warned of a crappy day ahead. It fit, he decided. Fit perfectly with the state of this case and his mood.

According to the phone's display he'd missed three calls, all from Heath. He punched in the number as soon as he was back inside with the door locked behind him. Having to make another sudden run for their lives this morning was not something he wanted to risk.

"It's me," he said when Heath answered the phone. He headed to the kitchen for another cup of coffee. "Yeah. I was tied up," he said in response to the comment about missed calls. He damn sure wasn't about to tell him just exactly how tied up he'd been.

Trent listened as Heath detailed the ruckus the feds were generating since the discovery of McCade's body. They wanted Trent and Kelly's location *ASAP*. Even the senator had been questioned extensively. The Chicago Bureau office was running interference on the Colby Agency's behalf. Trent wouldn't be able to put off turning Kelly in for much longer. Damn, things were getting a little too hot.

"Call me the moment you break that code or get an address on that girlfriend," Trent told him. "I'm getting desperate down here."

He closed the phone and heaved a disgusted breath. They needed a break in this case. Anything to use as leverage. When he turned Kelly over to the feds, which he would have no choice but to do eventually, they needed a bargaining chip. The files for assurance of her safety above all else. But first they had to be able to prove there was something worth trading for in those files.

Heath needed more time.

But time was running out.

KELLY'S EYES fluttered open and she inhaled deeply, savoring the essence of Trent and sex that lingered on her sheets. She rolled over onto her back, biting her lower lip as she inventoried her various aches and pains. She hadn't had sex in a long time and she'd never had *sex* like that before.

She closed her eyes and relived those awesome moments. After they'd caught their breath, he'd carried her to the bed and started the frenzy all over again. She shivered, her body heating up, tightening at the vivid memories. There was definitely something to be said for an older man. In her opinion he was a god between the sheets.

As much as she hated to, she dragged herself out of bed, glanced back longingly one last time then headed for the shower. The scent of coffee wafted from downstairs and she resisted the urge to join her cowboy in the kitchen…on the table…the counter…or about anywhere else he suggested.

She shivered again as she passed through the French doors separating the master bath from her bedroom. She damn sure hoped he knew what he'd gotten himself into. Kelly twisted the knobs in the shower to start the spray of water. He'd made her fall in love with him practically overnight. She had every intention of seeing that he made this right. Over and over again, she mused as she stepped into the steamy glass enclosure.

Scarcely ten minutes later she finished toweling dry her hair and tugged on a pair of jeans and a sweater. It was colder today. She didn't have to step outside, her heating system's inability to keep her place warm was indication enough.

Before going downstairs she hesitated. She'd like to take one more crack at those files. She chewed her lip thoughtfully. Trent would most likely come looking for her eventually, but until then she could give it a shot. She hurried to her computer and logged on.

She'd gotten in about ten minutes worth of futility when her Internet server let her know that she had new mail. The move automatic, she clicked the icon and opened her e-mail box. Her gaze riveted to the sender's name. Her pulse shot into hyper mode.

Kelly, I'm coming for you.

Romeo.

"Trent!" She scrambled from her chair and rushed toward the stairs only to run headlong into a brick wall.

Trent.

He steadied her. "What's wrong?"

"Romeo emailed me again!"

"Log off," he snapped, making her jump.

She backed away from him, bumping into her desk in the process. "I just…"

"Log off *now*," he repeated. "He can track your location that way."

Her heart thundering, she logged off, shut the computer down for good measure. He'd told her that…she remembered now. But she didn't quite understand. How could he track her that way? She spun around and stared up at Trent. "How can he do that?" She knew her Internet ID wasn't completely secure...but how could he know where she'd logged on from?

"It's like running a trace on a telephone line. It's simple." He hissed a curse. "I explained it to you before. Too late now. We need to get moving. We can't risk that he'll show up here any minute now."

She nodded and hurried back to her room for her shoes. She'd screwed up...again. But she'd only been online for a few minutes. Maybe that's all it took. The idea of having to outrun the hit man this morning was too much to bear. She was sick and tired of running...of being afraid.

By the time she got downstairs, Trent was ready to go. He shoved a cup of coffee at her. "I thought you might need this."

The heat from the cup and the heavenly smell was comforting. "Thanks." She grabbed her purse and followed him to the door. She was so sick of running. When they would have walked out, the ringing of the telephone halted their progress. They exchanged a look and by mutual unspoken agreement listened for the answering machine to pick up.

"I know you're there, Kelly. I'm coming for you."

Kelly felt the blood leech from her face. The voice was different...not the shooter. But, the threat was the same. He was coming. He or they wouldn't stop until she was dead. What was the point in running? There was no way to stop them. She didn't even know what he or the others looked like...wouldn't see them coming. No matter how long it took, she knew with deadly certainty that they would simply keep coming after her.

"Let's go!"

The order filtered through the trance she'd slipped into and Kelly jerked to attention. She had to trust Trent for now. He'd promised to protect her. He was her only chance. They'd shared more than their bodies last night, they'd shared everything.

As she climbed into the rental car next to him, another thought crashed into her. But who would protect him?

His cell phone buzzed. He flipped it open as he pulled out onto the street. She sipped her coffee, careful not to let it slosh over the side of the cup. She couldn't think about that…not right now. Her emotions were too raw.

"Is she in New Orleans?"

Kelly perked up then. Darlene, Ray's girlfriend, was supposed to be in New Orleans. Anticipation zipped through Kelly. She could have information. Otherwise why would she have taken off? She was afraid, just like Kelly. Why hadn't she thought of that already?

"We're on our way," Trent told his caller.

She waited as he dropped his phone into the seat for him to tell her what he'd learned.

He glanced at her, then slowed the car and executed a U-turn. "We're going to San Antonio."

Her brow furrowed in confusion. "What's in San Antonio? Was that call about Darlene?"

"A New Orleans detective spoke to her parents.

Darlene isn't with them, she's hiding out in San Antonio at an old friend's place. She wants to talk to you.'' Trent's gaze locked with hers for just one second before he turned his attention back to the street. ''Only you.''

THE DRIVE to San Antonio took close to three hours. They didn't talk much. Mostly about the sun's unexpected appearance and her parents. Trent could hear the love in her voice. They'd been a truly close-knit family. Not like his. His folks had retired to Florida years ago. Both his sisters lived in California. They rarely called each other, saw each other even less often. But he stayed busy with work so he hadn't really noticed.

Until now.

Until she made him think about home and family and…other things he'd promised himself he wouldn't think about anytime soon. Taking care of a family required a great deal of time. His work kept him away from home a lot. It was, at times like now, dangerous. What kind of life was that for a family?

A family they could have very well started last night. Though they'd used a condom the first go around, things had gotten even more out of control after that and the entire concept of prevention had vanished from his mind. He hadn't been able to think of anything else but her.

It wasn't that he didn't want children…and a wife, he just hadn't expected to want either of them now. His gaze was inexplicably drawn to her. He wanted her. His body reacted instantly to the thought.

He shook his head at his own weakness. And all this time he'd considered himself a tough guy.

"That's the street!" Kelly pointed to the next right.

Trent took the turn and slowly cruised down the residential street looking for house number 247. He eased over to the curb in front of the small Craftsman bungalow.

"I should check it out first," Trent said, eyeing the too quiet house suspiciously. Heath had insisted that it was safe, but still...

"She said just me."

Dammit, he didn't want her going in there alone. "Kelly, I don't—"

She placed a hand on his arm. "I know you don't like this. Neither do I. But I have to."

His next move startled him as much as it did her. He took her face in his hands and kissed her. He couldn't bear the thought of losing her...of her being hurt in any way. He drew back, released her reluctantly. "I still don't like it," he muttered.

"I liked it a lot," she said teasingly, speaking, of course, about the kiss.

When she reached for the door handle he stopped her with a hand on her arm. "I want you to take this." He drew his Glock from its holster. "You take it off safety right here."

She stared at the gun for a moment then shook her head. "I've never even held one."

He put the weapon in her hand. "You have now."

She nodded jerkily, then shoved it into her purse.

Trent got out of the car and leaned against it as she walked up to the door. She was nervous, he could see that, but she didn't let it stop her. She was something. A new kind of respect for her sprouted inside him.

Kelly moistened her lips and knocked on the door. She flexed her fingers and ordered her hands to stop shaking. Everything would be fine. She knew Darlene. There was no reason to be afraid…or nervous.

The door opened a crack. "You alone?" Darlene asked, her voice rusty from an obvious lack of sleep and years of indulging her cigarette habit.

"No," Kelly admitted. "I have a friend at the car." She gestured over her shoulder. "If you don't mind, I'd like him to join us. He's a private detective, he's trying to help me figure this out."

The one eye Kelly could see narrowed. "You sure you can trust him."

A smile moved across Kelly's lips before she could stop it. "Yeah," she said. "I know I can trust him."

"Well, tell him to come on then."

Kelly motioned to Trent that it was okay for him to come. He didn't hesitate.

Darlene opened the door and allowed them inside. "Have a seat," she said, eyeing Trent speculatively. She closed and bolted the door.

"I'm glad you survived, kid," she said to Kelly as she lit a cigarette. "Now tell me about your friend here."

"His name is Trent Tucker. He's with the Colby Agency in Chicago. Senator Lester hired him to find out what really happened to…" She swallowed, hard. "What happened to Ray."

Darlene's expression hardened and she shifted her gaze to Trent. "I'll tell you what happened," she said harshly. "They killed him to keep him from telling what he knew."

"Ms. Whitehead," Trent began gently, "what exactly did Ray know? Anything you can share will help us fight these people."

Darlene sat down on the arm of a chair facing their position on the sofa. "What I know might get you killed," she said bluntly before exhaling a cloud of blue smoke.

Kelly clasped her hands in her lap to keep from fidgeting. "I…" she cleared her throat. "I have the files from the disk Ray gave me."

"That disk got him killed," Darlene said grimly, turning her attention to Kelly. "He knew he'd made a mistake shortly after taking on that client."

"Be as specific as you can," Trent urged. "I know this is difficult, but the details are extremely important."

Darlene stubbed out her cigarette in a nearby ashtray and shifted from the arm of the chair to the seat. She looked exhausted. Dark rings underscored her eyes and her skin looked far too pale. Kelly had lost a great boss, but Darlene had lost the man she loved. This had to be immensely difficult. Kelly felt for her.

"About a year ago Ray took on this new client, the Renaissance Corporation."

Kelly's heart started to beat faster.

"The proposition they made him was too good to be true and he knew it." Darlene lifted a shoulder in a weary shrug. "But he couldn't resist. It seemed pretty much harmless. Until they started to demand all these pointless market moves. Ray tried to tell them that it was a waste of time and their money, but they insisted. He knew it was just a matter of time before the feds noticed the way he was handling those accounts. Nobody legit makes maneuvers like that. He wanted out.''

"When did he first mention wanting out?" Trent prodded.

"About six months ago." She looked at Kelly again. "About the same time he hired you."

That's why she'd never worked on those accounts, he'd started keeping them separate by that time. It made sense now, Kelly realized.

"Then this woman, Ann Jones, showed up," Darlene went on.

Uneasiness slid through Kelly at the mention of Ann's name. She'd been her friend, someone she trusted.

"Ray knew she was keeping tabs on him for the cartel.''

"The cartel?" Trent cut in. "He believed this Renaissance was connected to the cartel?"

"Sure." She reached for her pack of cigarettes and lit another one. "It's all in the files. Names, everything.''

"But I haven't been able to interpret it. It's just a bunch of numbers.''

"Look at it again," Darlene told her. "I don't know anything about it, but Ray said that it read the way an account should read.''

Kelly thought about that a moment and decided she wasn't sure she understood. But even more troubling to her was the news about her friend. "You're positive Ann worked for the cartel?'' Kelly still didn't want to believe the worst about her.

Darlene held her hands palms up. ''Beats the hell out of me, but that's what Ray thought.''

''What about the FBI agent?'' Trent pressed. ''Was he blackmailing Ray in some way?''

She frowned. ''What do you mean?''

''The H.P.D. detective investigating the case found an envelope from Ray's firm containing twenty-five thousand in cash in the agent's jacket pocket.''

That just couldn't be right. Kelly and Darlene exchanged a glance before she took a long drag of tar and nicotine. ''We're talking about the guy from Dallas, Agent Davis?''

Trent nodded.

''That's a load of crap. Ray hadn't ever met the guy before. He'd been meeting with one of the local feds for two months. Thought the guy was giving him the runaround.'' She made a scoffing sound. ''Soon as Ray got his nerve up he went to the feds, told 'em what he suspected. The agent insisted they needed tangible evidence. So Ray started compiling the proof he needed to bring the cartel down. It was never enough for that fed. So Ray called someone from the Dallas office. They were going to meet that evening…last Friday.'' Her voice quavered and trailed off.

''Do you remember the Houston agent's name?'' Trent asked when she didn't say more.

She nodded. ''Sure. It was McCade. Agent McCade.''

Kelly and Trent looked at each other, both thinking

the same thing. McCade had been a setup. The shooter had used him to lure them to that club. And he'd tied up one more loose end in the process.

"I just have one question for you, Mr. P.I.," Darlene said to Trent. He looked back at her expectantly. "Can you get the bastard who killed my Ray?"

Trent smiled, it wasn't pleasant. "Damn straight, ma'am. I won't stop until I do."

She nodded, satisfied with his response.

Anxiety tightened around Kelly's chest. Ann had a part in this...in Ray's murder. Their friendship had probably been part of her job, nothing more. She couldn't help feeling sad at the idea. How could she have been so blind? So naive?

"Ms. Whitehead," Trent was saying, drawing Kelly's attention back to the conversation, "I'm not sure you're entirely safe here. If we could find you, we have to assume that the killer can find you as well."

"I'm not going to the police or the feds," she protested. "After what happened to Ray, I don't trust 'em."

Kelly could definitely understand that, she felt the same way herself. Except she knew it wasn't the police in general, nor was it the whole FBI. There was simply a bad element in Houston and they didn't know the good guys from the bad guys just yet.

"I'd like to suggest that you let one of my people keep you safe until we know who we can trust in Houston," Trent offered. "All it will take is one phone call. I can put you on a plane to Chicago and he'll be waiting on the other end."

She sucked long and deep on her smoke before responding. "I guess I could use a little vacation. What's it like in Chicago this time of year? Got snow up there?"

Whatever Trent said in answer was lost on Kelly. It was at that precise moment that she knew just how deep into trouble she was and it had nothing to do with the threat of death hanging over her head.

"You always lived in Chicago?" Darlene carried on with her inquisition. "Hell, I thought you were a Texas fella when I saw you propped against that car."

What Trent said to that was unimportant. Chicago was his home. That's where he'd come from when he'd showed up at her door. That's where he'd go back to when this was over. She was just a case...a case that had gotten personal.

Too personal.

He might have feelings for her...but they would never be enough.

WHEN THEY'D PUT Darlene on a Chicago bound commuter flight and headed back to Houston, Trent turned his attention back to the matter at hand: Keeping Kelly safe until they figured out who they could trust. But mere protection wasn't enough.

Decoding those files was imperative. If the files contained the right evidence and combined with the girlfriend's testimony and with what Kelly knew, they could nail the cartel. The senator would be pleased.

But the shooter was another subject altogether. He was likely contracted. Someone outside the cartel.

Catching him would be a whole other ball of wax. Even if he kept Kelly and Darlene safe until the cartel was brought down through the legal system there was still the concern as to the hit man's reputation. He apparently didn't work alone. Kelly hadn't recognized the voice when he'd left that threatening message. The whole team they'd encountered at Jarvis's office the night it burned down was obviously fully involved.

Though the shooters could walk away clean, since they were likely not associated with the cartel on that level, Kelly's survival was a black mark on the team's record, or the leader's at the very least. A failure. If the man was any kind of professional, as Trent suspected, he would want to erase that mark.

Bottom line: Kelly wouldn't be safe until the bastard was behind bars...or dead.

Either way would be fine with Trent, as long as the matter was taken care of.

Trent glanced over at his passenger. She'd been oddly quiet since they'd left the airport. Not that he could blame her for feeling down, she had just learned that her best friend had deceived her. He imagined she felt completely alone.

He didn't want her to feel that way. But she looked so unapproachable at the moment, he hesitated to reach out to her. To hell with it, he had to follow his instincts.

When he would have taken her hand in his, his cell buzzed. He snatched it up and popped it open.

"Tucker."

It was Heath. He damn sure hoped he had good news for him this time. He glanced at Kelly. She needed to hear something good.

"We broke the code. I'm printing out the results now. Where are you?"

"About an hour from Houston," Trent told him, as he moved smoothly around a truck and trailer loaded with brand-new cars.

"Don't go back to Ms. Pruitt's apartment," Heath warned. "Apparently there was a break-in, the cops were called and the feds are watching the place in hopes you two will come back there."

"We'll go to the hotel we stayed in night before last. Fax me a copy of those files." He reminded him of the hotel's name and the alias he'd used there. "I want Kelly to look them over as soon as possible."

"Will do. Listen Trent," Heath said solemnly, "you need to be careful, man. These guys are big guns."

Trent didn't doubt that for a moment. Two federal agents were dead already.

"Keep me informed," Heath urged before hanging up to run to the airport to meet Darlene Whitehead.

Trent tossed his phone into the seat and scrubbed a hand over his face. It was time he and the senator had a face-to-face. The only problem was, how would he get Kelly to agree to stay out of the line of fire?

Images from last night's incredible lovemaking flickered through his worrisome thoughts. And how in hell was he going to make her his when this was over?

Damn, he'd fallen hard. Too bad she was still hung up on all that he'd walked away from when he left Texas.

And Chicago was a long way from Texas.

Chapter Fourteen

Kelly sat in the middle of the king-size bed poring over the pages Heath had faxed to the hotel. Trent had ordered room service, sans the champagne, and she nibbled on a chocolate covered strawberry as she considered the data.

Trent paced the room, doing his damnedest not to look at her. Every time those luscious lips nestled around one of those strawberries he almost groaned. He blew out a breath and paced some more. Maybe if he paced long enough to wear down this instantaneous physical reaction now bulging in his jeans he could think past what he wanted to do to her. How he wanted to taste her...lick and nibble on her like she was doing those damned berries.

"How clever," she murmured. "Ray, you were far smarter than I gave you credit."

Trent cleared his throat and sat down on the edge of the bed to get a look at the information for himself. She'd snatched it from the clerk before he could grab it. He could certainly understand her eagerness. Those documents held the key to her getting her life back.

A life that might not include him.

He shook off the thought. A case. An assignment. This was work. He had to remember that.

"See what he did," she pointed to the numeric codes that had baffled them from the start. "These numbers specify the account, the dates and amounts of activities. Then, these numbers stand for letters of the alphabet. The numbers represent a state. See this, it's Kentucky, the fifteenth state admitted into the union. The corresponding fifteenth letter of the alphabet is O. Eventually you spell out Oglesby."

The name set off an alarm in Trent's brain. "Oglesby as in Governor Oglesby?"

She looked at the name again. "Unless there's another Hezekiah Oglesby who hails from Houston, Texas."

The senator had suggested the governor was dirty. Was that why the FBI was involved? Did Oglesby have someone under his thumb?

"And look here." She pointed to another page. "Here he lists all the times he met with McCade and the promises he made. It's incredible."

Well that answered one question. And she was right. It was incredible in content and simplicity, Trent thought. Ray Jarvis had no training, not even a vague idea of how to set up an unbreakable code, but he'd succeeded in slowing down even the professionals. Fear and desperation were serious motivators.

"Heath has turned over a copy to the senator by now," Trent commented, more a thought spoken. "We should be hearing from him soon."

"Is this enough?" Kelly asked, her expression

turning worried, the excitement of the breakthrough wearing off now.

"It should be enough," Trent assured her. "With this and Darlene's testimony, it should discredit all those involved at the very least. The lives they've known until now will forever change whether with a jail sentence or simply due to loss of credibility with the public." The governor, politically speaking, was a dead man.

The silence thickened between them and Trent suddenly wished he hadn't gotten so close. He had to get this case back on track. Distraction could be a dangerous thing. Had already taken a toll...one she might not even be aware of. They'd crossed the line last night, there was no taking that move back. He straightened away from her, putting some distance between them.

She sat there for a moment, then pushed the papers aside and looked directly into his eyes. "This is about last night, isn't it?"

The underlying sadness in her eyes almost undid him. How could he make her understand without hurting her? His actions just now had already done damage. He hadn't wanted this...hadn't wanted to hurt her in any way. She was so vulnerable, more so than even she realized. That he'd taken advantage of that vulnerability was wrong. He should have been stronger than that.

"You think it was a mistake?" She lifted her chin in defiance of her own statement. She didn't want to hear him echo those words, but she had to know what was on his mind. He read her so well.

"A mistake is an error, something you didn't intend to do…something you regret." He let her see in his eyes the overwhelming emotions ripping him apart inside. "My only regret is in timing."

She looked away. "I understand."

He wasn't sure she did. If she truly understood she would know that last night had forever changed his tomorrows. Nothing would ever be the same. And somehow he had to make that right for her and him.

"Kelly—"

His cell phone interrupted the additional explanation he believed the subject required. He wanted her to know that she was no one-night stand to him. What had happened between them was special.

"Tucker," he said impatiently.

"The senator wants to meet with the two of you now. He's poised to take this public but there are a few things he needs to clarify with Kelly first."

Trent swore silently. He didn't feel good about giving away their position until they'd figured out a way to get to the shooters. Their names weren't on that damned list of who's-who among greedy drug peddlers. Oh, sure, those guys never sullied their hands with the actual merchandise, they simply made sure the money was in place…pristine and untraceable.

"Where?"

Heath gave him a location that was both quiet and out of the way, offering the perfect climate for a setup. "Tell him the answer is no. If he wants to meet with me, I'll be watching for him at the food court of the Galleria."

Heath brought him up to speed on Darlene Whitehead's whereabouts and they ended the call with a final urge from Heath that he be very careful.

"So, when do we leave?"

Kelly was up and tugging on her shoes.

"You should stay here," he told her, knowing the coming argument would be pointless. Outside his tying her up and locking her in the bathroom, she would insist on going.

"You know that isn't going to happen." She glanced at the place beneath his jacket where his weapon nestled against his side. "Unless you intend to use force."

She knew that wasn't going to happen.

Her determination and resilience never ceased to amaze him. "All right, let's discuss our strategy."

THE STUNNING architecture of the fifth largest mall in the nation provided little comfort as Kelly followed Trent to the second floor balcony overlooking the food court. She'd been here dozens of times but never had her heart pounded and her palms sweat as they did now.

But then, she looked up at Trent, she'd never been here with this man before. Admittedly, it was more than his presence. She was scared…just a little. She'd be pretty stupid not to be. But determination had pretty much outmuscled the fear. She wanted this over. She wanted justice. She wanted to know if this cowboy she'd fallen so hard for would walk away when his case was closed.

It wasn't fair not to give him any warning that she was analyzing his every move, but life wasn't always fair. She needed to know how he really felt. Not what his guilty conscience goaded him into saying or feeling. She wanted the truth. Truth had always been extremely important to her, even when she wasn't telling it.

Trent had stopped by a boutique near the hotel to pick up their camouflage. Kelly, after all, was a fugitive, her face still being flashed on the news. And the senator would recognize Trent. Not to mention the cops and feds likely had his description, too.

Surprise had to be on their side. They didn't need any surprises from the other side. This thing could still go either way. And one of them could still end up dead.

That was the part that worried her the most.

Trent leaned on the railing, pulling her close to his side. "Just relax and pretend you're enjoying the view."

Oh, the view was magnificent from her vantage. But she had a feeling he was talking about the Galleria, not his chiseled profile. He wore his cowboy hat pulled down low, shadowing his face. He'd traded in her Girl Power black T-shirt for a cotton button-down shirt and a denim jacket that looked good with his jeans. She wore a brunette wig. He'd picked out skin-tight black jeans for her and a black cashmere sweater that had no doubt set him back a pretty penny. She wondered if he would be reimbursed for his trouble.

After all, this was work. She was his assignment and, in all likelihood, a hefty tax write-off the way he was throwing around cash in his effort to take care of her.

He had said his only regret was timing, but was that just a nice guy's way of letting her down easy?

She pushed the thoughts away. She couldn't think about that right now. It hurt too much. Her emotions were still fragile from last night. Nothing about her would ever be strong enough to help her forget the feelings he'd brought to life in her.

Except her resolve to see that he didn't get himself killed trying to protect her.

Trent spotted the senator within minutes of their arrival at the Galleria. But he made him wait. For more than an hour he watched him, a single occupant at a table for four, a soft drink melting on the Formica top. No one had approached him or made any kind of overt contact with him. He appeared to be alone.

"How much longer are we going to wait?"

It was the first time she'd questioned him since they arrived. Like the senator, she'd reached the end of her patience.

"Until," Trent said, "right now."

The senator pushed out of his chair and stalked to a trash receptacle and deposited his untouched drink there. Trent, with Kelly right behind him, took the escalator down, keeping the senator in his line of sight.

His stride impatient, the politician moved toward the exit on the other side of the food court. The senator wasn't accustomed to being kept waiting.

But Trent had to be sure…at least as sure as he could be.

They stayed several meters behind him, careful not to close in too fast. Trent stalled when the senator abruptly took a right into a long corridor marked Rest Rooms.

The hair on the back of his neck stood on end and he knew he'd been had.

He pulled Kelly close. "We're going to make a run for it."

"What?" She looked up at him, confusion troubling her expression. "I don't—"

"Follow the route the senator took, Mr. Tucker."

The male voice behind him was accompanied by the nudge of a muzzle in his spleen.

Trent didn't bother to respond. The man had a distinct advantage. He gripped Kelly's shoulders tightly, ready to propel her away from them as they made the turn into the corridor. The momentary distraction of the crowd would give her a chance to run if she didn't blow it waiting for him.

Now or never. As he turned into the corridor he readied to give Kelly a hard shove but she twisted away from him.

"Who the hell are you?" she demanded of the man behind them. "What do you want?"

Trent whipped around and attempted to get her behind him. That the man hadn't fired his weapon puzzled him but he didn't have time to wonder at the moment. "Kelly—"

She shoved the heel of her hand into the man's chest. "Tell me what you want, dammit!"

"I'm a federal agent," he said quickly. "DEA!"

He pulled his hand from his jacket pocket, the one where he'd concealed the gun and reached into his interior pocket. At Trent's reaction he held up his free hand. "I'm getting my ID that's all." He flashed his Drug Enforcement Agency identification. Allan Benson. "I need to speak with you, Ms. Pruitt. It's imperative that we do this now."

Relaxing a fraction, Trent took Kelly by the arm before she assaulted the man further. "You have an office in here?" he said pointedly, nodding toward the corridor.

The man shrugged. "In a manner of speaking."

He led the way, pausing at a door marked Maintenance. He knocked twice and the door opened.

"What took you so long?"

Senator Lester, looking entirely flustered, waited in the cramped room that held janitorial supplies, mops, brooms and the like.

"We have everything under control now," Agent Benson assured him.

"What do you want?" Kelly repeated. She was sick to death of this sneaking around stuff. This guy had better start talking fast.

Trent tried to conceal a grin but wasn't quite successful. She didn't see a damned thing funny about it. Senator Lester just stood there, looking baffled.

"I contacted the senator today when the Houston FBI office let me know there had been a break in the case."

"The files," Lester explained. "I was preparing to fax the files to the special agent in charge there when he insisted I come in to the office." Lester looked from Kelly and Trent to Benson and back. "I had no idea DEA was in on this. That's why the FBI has behaved so strangely. They were trying to protect their ongoing investigation. They knew McCade was dirty and that Davis had been set up.''

Benson picked it up from there. ''We had an agent under deep cover within the cartel's framework for quite some time. Unfortunately that agent was killed before we could get our hands on the needed files.'' He looked directly at Kelly then. ''If I understand the senator correctly, you are the only connection to the shooter we have.''

She nodded, too shaken to speak. What agent? Who was he talking about? ''But I think there's more than one.''

''That's possible. Right now I need your help, Ms. Pruitt,'' Agent Benson pressed. ''That bastard killed one of our best agents, I want him. I want him bad.''

''What agent?'' She shook her head, confusion churning. She had no idea what he was talking about.

''Agent Anna Dixon. You know her as Ann Jones.''

The breath went out of Kelly and the only thing that kept her vertical was Trent's strong arm darting out to catch her when she swayed. ''Ann?'' she murmured, scarcely able to say the name.

He nodded, his expression grim. ''I believe she died trying to protect you from the assassin she knew had been ordered to take out Jarvis.''

Kelly couldn't listen to any more. She turned her face into Trent's solid chest and tried to hold back the tears...tried to think how this could have been true and her not know it.

''Mr. Tucker, I realize Ms. Pruitt has been through a horrific ordeal already,'' Benson went on. ''The files she was able to get out of Jarvis's office will destroy the cartel. That's a done deal. In fact, arrest warrants are being drawn up as we speak.''

''What is it you want, Benson?'' Trent demanded gruffly. Kelly felt the sharpness of his words rumble in his chest.

''The assassin or assassins know she survived. He's going to want to take care of that loose end—''

''Tell us something we don't know,'' Trent snapped, cutting him off. ''Let me tell you something I know.'' His deadly tone startled Kelly, sent a chill racing up her spine. ''I know what you're getting at. You've lost a fellow agent. You want revenge. You want the killer. I can't blame you. But I won't let you use Kelly to get him. Do I make myself clear?''

She went still…ice forming in her veins.

''Very clear,'' Benson said wearily. ''But let me remind you of something I'm quite certain you know, he won't stop. You know it and so do I. She won't ever be safe as long as he's alive.''

Kelly squeezed her eyes shut and blocked out the rest of his words. He was right. She hadn't needed him to tell her. Her life would never be her own if the killer, killers, she amended, weren't brought down. She was living on borrowed time.

She opened her eyes and peered up at Trent. And so was he as long as he was acting as her protector.

TRENT PACED the hotel room much as he'd done earlier that day, unable to sit, too furious to discuss the issue further with Kelly.

She wouldn't listen to reason.

Too hardheaded to be swayed, she was determined to go through with Benson's cockamamie plan. Hell yeah, he might just nail the bad guys, but at what price?

Trent didn't like it. He didn't like it at all.

But nothing he'd said had changed her mind. Benson had discovered that McCade had himself an H.P.D. cop in his pocket, a Detective Kennamer. The guy had caved during interrogation, swearing he hadn't done anything other than pass along information. To make it easier on himself he had agreed to play messenger one last time. He would pass a certain message to a member of the cartel who would in turn call in their clean-up man, the man in charge of taking out Jarvis and his assistant and anyone else the cartel deemed necessary. Dammit. This was far too dicey for comfort. No matter how much backup they had in place, DEA and FBI as well as several Houston cops including Detective Hargrove, the shooter could still kill her.

"It's time," Kelly announced, exiting the bathroom with the female agent Benson had sent over to suit her up for this late night rendezvous.

"Mr. Tucker, did you put on your vest?" the agent asked.

He rolled his eyes and heaved a disgusted breath. "Yeah, yeah, I put it on."

Kelly wore a Kevlar vest and a wire. But neither of those things would stop a bullet to the head.

Dammit all to hell why wouldn't she listen to reason?

"I'll…ah…give you two a moment," the agent offered, obviously noting Trent's agitation. "I'll be in the corridor."

"Don't say it," Kelly ordered before he could even speak. "I have to do this. You know I do. It won't be over until he's caught."

She wanted to be strong. But he could see right through her. She was scared to death. "You don't have to do this," he urged, moving closer, needing to be nearer to her. "There are other ways. They could send in a female agent in your place. Someone trained to take this kind of risk."

She shook her head. "He would know. He's a professional. You said so yourself."

Trent swore, hotly, repeatedly.

"You're not going to change my mind." She folded her arms over her chest and stared up at him defiantly. "Now kiss me and play nice."

Trent closed his eyes and heaved an anxiety riddled sigh. "I wish you would listen to me."

"Just kiss me, cowboy," she urged, drawing him closer. "And everything will be fine."

He cupped her face in his hands. "Leave with me right now and I'll be that cowboy you're looking for. I'll find a way to—"

"Trent," she murmured softly, interrupting his desperate plea, "you're more than just a cowboy, you're my hero. You don't have to pretend. Besides, you can take the cowboy out of Texas, but you can't take Texas out of the cowboy. You grew up here. This will always be a part of you no matter how you try to pretend it's not. You are a cowboy and we've had a hell of a ride. Don't make me any promises right now. Just kiss me."

He covered her mouth with his, needing to stop her before she said more of those words he couldn't bear to hear. The taste of her…the smell of her, sent emotion after emotion ripping through his chest. He couldn't lose her…

"I'm sorry," the female DEA agent interrupted. "We have to go now."

Trent stared down at Kelly's angelic face and made a silent promise that he would keep if it killed him. No way was she going to be hurt tonight.

Not on his watch.

KELLY TIGHTENED the sash on her robe and fluffed the pillows on her bed. She surveyed her bedroom, careful not to allow her gaze to linger on the saddle. She'd put everything back in place. Whoever had gone through her town house while she and Trent had gone to San Antonio hadn't done too much damage. Mostly pulled things out of drawers and generally misplaced her stuff.

"Ms. Pruitt, can you hear me okay in there?"

The voice echoed from the communications earpiece she wore. She coughed twice in response to the question.

Those were her instructions. Cough twice for yes or if all was well, clear her throat for no or if she was in trouble.

Kennamer had delivered the message that since the Bureau now had possession of the files that Kelly deemed it safe to go back home. Trent Tucker had gone back to Chicago and the cartel would be history very soon. Agent Benson was banking on the assassin, hit man or men, coming back to clear up the one final loose end after receiving that message. For good measure Benson had added that Jarvis had confessed all to Kelly and that she would be testifying in the case against the cartel.

If that didn't lure the killer to her, nothing would.

Trent had gone ballistic. A tingle zinged from her belly all the way to her heart. He'd been willing to offer her anything if she'd back off. That pleased her immensely but it also annoyed her. Those promises needed to be made out of love not fear. She'd wanted him out of harm's way but he'd raised so much hell that Benson had finally gone along with his being close at hand to aid Kelly.

She strolled to the master bath and turned off the water filling her whirlpool tub. "Hardheaded jerk," she muttered as she surveyed the mound of fluffy bubbles prepared for a luxurious bath. Too bad they would have to wait until after she'd parlayed with the killer. She'd already had to add more to the mix twice.

What if the bastard didn't show?

She wrapped her arms around her middle and padded back into her bedroom. He had to show. She wanted this over. She wanted the man who had killed Ann and Ray to pay dearly. His partner, too. She thought of that voice on her answering machine.

An ache swelled in her chest as she thought of her dear friend. No wonder she hadn't kept any personal documents at her condo. Her whole identity had been a cover profile. Kelly swiped at a tear as she thought of how her friend had kicked that disk under her desk to protect her. She had knowingly taken the bullet intended for Kelly.

Ann was a hero and she damned sure hadn't deserved to die at the hand of some scumbag killer. Kelly would never know why Ann had come to the office that fateful evening unarmed. She could have taken the guy down. Agent Benson speculated that she hadn't wanted to blow the operation. Or that she'd expected the shooter to recognize her and think she was supposed to oversee the hit. DEA had never before gotten anyone that deep.

"Heads up, people." Benson's voice in her ear. "We have company."

However brave Kelly had thought herself to be when she insisted on doing this, fear, stark and vivid, coursed through her veins upon hearing those words. She clung to her waning anger, used it to solidify her courage.

She moved around her bedroom, pretending to go about preparing for bed. She dragged her fingers across the sleek leather saddle and remembered how wonderful it had felt to have Trent filling her so completely.

There had to be a future for them…somehow.

"He's in the house. One man. His four-man backup team has taken up positions outside."

That final warning from Benson sent her into the master bath. That room was monitored, audio and video. There was an agent in her closet, under her bed, and in the linen closet directly across from the toilet. Not to mention a half dozen others hidden about downstairs. Another group of agents posted outside would take care of the hit man's backup team, but not until they had what they needed.

She closed her eyes and imagined Trent's face once more. He was close by, too. As frightening as this was…they had to end this now.

She forced herself to go through the ritual of brushing her teeth. The steam in the room from the waiting tub of hot water and frothy bubbles pressed in on her. Her heart beat faster and faster. *Please God, don't let him hurt anyone here tonight. Keep us safe. We just need to finish this.*

"Well, well, isn't this sweet?"

Though she had known he was in the house, that his appearance in her room was imminent, she still gasped. She dropped her toothbrush and turned to stare at the man standing in the middle of her bedroom. It was the one who'd left the threatening message…not the one she'd heard in the office…not the original shooter. She would never forget that voice. Was this man the head honcho? Was the other one outside? Her pulse reacted to the idea that he might get away. She didn't want that. He had to pay.

The French doors that separated her master bath and the bedroom stood open wide, leaving no barriers between her and this killer.

"Who are you?" The words came out weak, breathless, terrified. She swallowed, tried to slow the harsh pounding in her chest. She had to be stronger than this. Everyone was counting on her.

The weapon leveled at her face didn't waver as he

moved toward her. The vest wouldn't help her if he fired now. "Nice saddle," the bastard commented dryly. She couldn't see his face. He wore a ski mask as the men the other night who'd broken into Ray's office had. He wore those same black combat style clothes and the boots. Even the gloves were the same.

"You killed Ray and Ann. You have the disk. Why don't you leave me alone?" she demanded, allowing her voice to rise naturally with the panic welling inside her. "What do you want from me?" She leaned against the vanity for support and to remind her to stay in place. She couldn't deviate from the plan. There was no margin for error.

"I think you know what I want." He moved closer...almost to the French doors now. He tugged off his mask and looked directly into her eyes.

Her breath stalled in her throat. His head was shaved close, almost to the point of baldness. Those dark eyes were wide-spaced and sinister-looking. But it was the evil tilt of his lips that unnerved her the most. That he wanted her to see his face was not good...indicated his lack of fear.

"I only have one question for you before I finish this," he said cruelly. "Where were you hiding that night?" he urged, giving his gun a little wave. "I'm intrigued by your resourcefulness."

"You don't know?" she asked, her voice a little shakier than she would have liked. "Haven't you considered the only place you didn't look?" she added with a hint of challenge, knowing he couldn't possibly know. The voice in her communications earpiece warned her not to get too cocky.

The scumbag laughed, the sound menacing. "Unfortunately I wasn't there that night. I think you know that. You need not concern yourself with the other man, however, since he proved incompetent. Not only did he miss you, but he killed Ann. For that he paid the ultimate price."

An unholy feeling of glee rushed through her at knowing her friends' killer was dead. Then, for just one second she was very nearly certain this man had felt something for Ann. He'd been the Romeo. She'd suspected as much but now she was suddenly certain. She suppressed the urge to tell him that Ann had been a federal agent, one poised to bring him down. Dragging this out might cause a deadly chain reaction. "So you do the cartel's dirty work," she suggested as per Benson's plan. She had to hold out just a little longer…get what they needed to tie this guy to the cartel with his own words.

He hummed a note of amusement. "The cartel would be nothing without me. I do damage control, like now. When they screw up, as they invariably do, I *undo*."

"It was Ann who helped me escape," she said tightly, her fingers clenching the marble vanity top so hard she feared it might just crack. She hadn't meant to say it…it just popped out. She needed him to know that he hadn't had any real control over Ann…she hadn't been one of them.

"I'm afraid I underestimated her allegiance to you. It's a shame really. I rather enjoyed playing Romeo to her Juliet."

It was all Kelly could do not to hurl herself at him

then and there. She wanted him to die. He didn't deserve a trial.

He sighed dramatically. "At any rate, it's time I finished the job. Whether the cartel goes down or not, I pride myself in my work."

Her eyes widened and the air evaporated in her lungs as he angled his head, taking aim. "Any last words before you go, pretty lady?"

Water and bubbles exploded from the whirlpool tub, pouring onto the tiled floor, spraying through the air. The killer swung his aim in that direction but too late.

Trent put a bullet right between his eyes.

The man dropped like a rock, the weapon still clutched in his hand.

Kelly crumbled to the wet floor, her legs refusing to hold her weight a second longer. He was dead. The man who had orchestrated the murders of her friends was dead. Thank God.

A soaking wet Trent rushed to her side while what looked like a dozen federal agents swarmed around the downed shooter. She could hear Benson ordering the takedown of the other men outside.

"You okay?" Trent collapsed onto the floor, dragging her into his lap. "You okay?" he demanded when she didn't respond immediately.

He was hot and wet and getting bubbles all over her. She wanted to laugh but she cried instead. Dammit. She'd been doing far too much of that lately.

"What do you think?" She trembled in spite of the heat emanating from his big strong body.

"I've got you," he murmured, his lips whispering

against her temple. "I'm here and I'm not going anywhere."

She drew back, looked up into his eyes. "You sure about that, cowboy? What about Chicago?"

One corner of that sexy mouth hitched into a smile. "I don't know, I thought maybe I'd try my hand at ranching." He kissed the tip of her nose. "Cattle, horses, the whole nine yards. I can always help the Colby Agency out from time to time."

She swiped a mass of bubbles from his jaw. "Are you sure about this?" Her heart stumbled…hesitated, then jumped for joy when he nodded resolutely.

"Well," she dragged out the word as if considering his offer. "Only if we can use my saddle on a very regular basis," she qualified.

He grinned, that sexy gleam in his eyes giving her an affirming answer even before he spoke. "Deal."

And then he kissed her and nothing else mattered. Except…

She drew back abruptly. "Wait!"

Everyone in the room jumped, startled by her outburst. She'd forgotten all about them until that moment. Her frantic gaze tangled with Trent's. "We have to go back to Galveston and find Felix." Taking care of Ann's beloved tomcat was the least she could do for her friend.

Trent smiled that smile that made her heart fly back into that acrobatic routine. "You mind if I dry off first?" he teased.

The hot, wet heat of his powerful body had already melted every ounce of fear from her body. The realization that they didn't have to run anymore…that they were safe finally sank through her whirling thoughts. "Take your time," she said, her entire demeanor suddenly calm. "There's no rush."

He cradled her face gently, oblivious to the official goings-on now resuming around them. "That's right. We've got the rest of our lives."

And then he kissed her again.

Epilogue

Victoria poured Ian another cup of tea, then carefully set the elegant china pot she'd inherited from her grandmother back on the matching tray.

"I'm glad we were able to take care of Senator Lester's situation," she said, sitting back in her chair and smiling at her two most trusted men, Ian Michaels and Simon Ruhl.

"It's official." Ian sipped his tea and set the cup and saucer aside. "Trent will be relocating to Texas to be with Kelly. They've already set a wedding date."

Victoria nodded. She hated to lose Trent, but she understood that kind of commitment. She would do most anything for Lucas...even consider his latest suggestion of settling the Leberman issue once and for all. Even in death he held one last secret over her head.

Simon commented, "I've scouted out two excellent potential investigators. I can move up the interview dates if you'd like. I think you'll be very pleased with their backgrounds. Either one or both would be assets to the agency.''

Lucas had wanted to be here for this meeting, but Victoria had needed to do this alone. ''That sounds fine, Simon.'' She took a deep breath and did what she had to do, as much as it pained her. ''I won't be returning to the office for a few more weeks.''

Ian and Simon exchanged a look. ''Is there an issue you wish to share?'' Ian prompted.

Never one to mince words, he'd likely sensed a problem the moment he walked in the door. ''As you are both aware, Lucas is convinced, and I must admit the newest evidence is compelling, that someone within our agency provided Leberman with crucial information.''

''I can't believe that,'' Simon argued with a shake of his head. ''No offense to Lucas, but we know the people he's talking about. It's impossible.''

''I agree,'' Victoria allowed to both men's amazement. ''However, I'm not fool enough to ignore the instincts of a man like Lucas.''

Neither man could deny that glaring fact.

''I believe that whoever has done this has done so unknowingly. That fact notwithstanding, it is essential that I know if such a breach has occurred. Especially in light of the most recent evidence Lucas has uncovered.''

''What evidence?'' Ian set his tea aside.

Victoria tamped down the emotions that tried to climb into her throat, making it difficult to breathe. This part was very nearly more than she could bear to say out loud. ''There was a second man involved in my son's disappearance. Lucas believes he is the one who played the part of watcher and provided necessary details which enabled Leberman to carry out his evil deeds.''

"Has he identified this man?"

"Yes. He's lining up the details now. We, of course, don't know where he is, but we do know where his daughter is. She's the only connection to him," she said in answer to Simon's next questions before he even asked.

"There's more," Ian suggested.

She had known he would see through her. "Yes, Ian, there is more."

She steeled her resolve and said the rest. "Since we can't be sure who has inadvertently been a party to Leberman's machinations, we have to assume it could be anyone."

She allowed them to digest that information before continuing. "And since we're in agreement that not one of us believes this can be possible, that discredits any objectivity we could hope to have in the situation."

Victoria knew by the looks on their faces that they suspected what she was about to say. "Lucas knows a man who has worked a number of years for the government. Always in the capacity as chief investigator of internal affairs. His reputation is unrivaled. He goes in with no preconceived notions and tells it like he sees it. Lucas trusts him, I trust Lucas. Do either of you have a problem with this?"

The silence thickened for a time.

Simon was the first to throw his hat into the ring.

"If this is what it takes to end Leberman's reign of terror, I'm all for it."

Victoria nodded in acknowledgement of his commitment.

"What's this man's name?" Ian wanted to know.

"Cole Danes. Have you heard of him?"

Ian contemplated his answer for a moment, then conceded, "I've heard of him. He's tough. No one will like him."

"Is it your impression then that this man is not to be trusted? That he isn't fair in his dealings?" Worry trickled through Victoria. She didn't want that kind of man taking over her agency even for a day.

Ian shook his head. "No, that would not be accurate. Cole Danes is more than fair. I have no doubt as to his dedication and loyalty. He simply has no bedside manner, so to speak."

Relief rushed through her. "Well, hopefully his mission won't take long." She looked from Ian to Simon and back. "So we have an understanding?"

"Yes," Ian agreed. "Cole Danes will conduct an internal affairs investigation which will put him in charge of the Colby Agency until further notice, starting…?"

He let the question hang in the air.

"Starting immediately," Victoria supplied.

And for the first time in more than twenty years someone else would be at the helm of the Colby Agency.

A man Victoria had never even met.

She prayed with all her heart that this would not be the beginning of the end.

The uncertainty was followed immediately by a feeling of inner strength and reassurance. She worried for nothing. Not only did she trust each and every member of her staff, she knew the Colby Agency had weathered worse. Nothing Cole Danes discovered could bring them down.

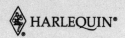

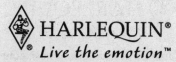

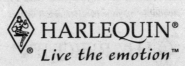

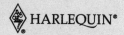

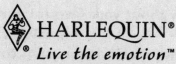

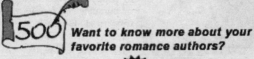

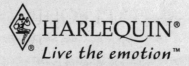

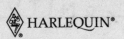
HARLEQUIN®

INTRIGUE

This summer, look for a Texas-sized series from three of your favorite authors...

Meting out the Texas law of the West on their own terms!

May 2004
OUT FOR JUSTICE
by *USA TODAY* bestselling author
Susan Kearney

June 2004
LEGALLY BINDING
Ann Voss Peterson

July 2004
LAWFUL ENGAGEMENT
Linda O. Johnston

Available at your favorite retail outlet.

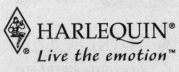
HARLEQUIN®
Live the emotion™

www.eHarlequin.com   HISC